Well Built

NEW YORK TIMES BESTSELLING AUTHORS

CARLY PHILLIPS
ERIKA WILDE

New York Times Bestselling Authors Carly Phillips and
Erika Wilde bring you a new fun, flirty, standalone romance.

When it comes to women, sexy, well-built Kyle Coleman
has always been a lover, not a fighter. His one exception?
The tempting, beautiful Ella Fisher. Her family and his
share a tempestuous past, which make the two of them as a
couple off-limits—despite the fact that she inspires some of
his dirtiest fantasies. He's kept his hands off of her for
years . . . until the lines between family loyalty and lust
become irrevocably blurred one fateful evening and changes
everything between them.

* * *

Chapter One

"**Y**OU DO REALIZE that you're about to start a major shit storm today, right?"

Kyle Coleman shifted his attention to Nolan Roberts, the man sitting in the passenger seat of his truck and his best friend since childhood. "Yes, I'm well aware that I'm about to piss off a certain someone who has no idea another person is interested in the run-down building next to her father's market," he replied to his friend, his tone droll. "Just like I know you're dying to witness everyone's shocked reaction when they realize *who* purchased the place, so don't fucking pretend you're accompanying me because you enjoy my sparkling personality."

Nolan merely smirked in response, silently admitting culpability.

When Kyle had mentioned attending today's public auction to Nolan, his friend had insisted on accompanying him. Not for moral support. No, Nolan's interest was all about witnessing the controversial purchase Kyle intended to make today. No matter the cost. Which meant outbidding Ella Fisher for the commercial piece of property she was also interested in. And because Kyle didn't want to give his rival any advance notice that she had competition for the building, Ella had no clue she was about to be blindsided.

Admittedly, a part of him felt guilty about the element of surprise he had in his favor, and there was no doubt in his mind Ella was going to be livid when he won the auction. But business was business, and Kyle wasn't about to treat this deal any differently just because he shared a tempestuous past with the woman who wanted the same piece of real estate that he did.

So, yeah, a major shit storm was about to touch down in his old hometown, as Nolan had so eloquently stated.

After his pronouncement, Nolan left Kyle to his thoughts as he continued to drive. He hit the outskirts of town, well aware that his brand-new, shiny red Ford F-250 was turning curious heads as he slowly drove the speed limit along the main street—appropriately *named* Main St.—which led through his hometown of Woodmont, Illinois, population 956, according to the welcome sign posted just outside the city limits. Considering the wide-eyed stares as he passed the various stores and the people strolling along the sidewalk, you'd think that he was driving a Bentley instead. But he knew the unique color of his truck, not to mention the rumbling sound of his diesel engine, was enough to alert everyone in town that an outsider was driving through.

He gripped his fingers tighter on the steering wheel as he headed toward his destination. For his entire childhood, he'd felt like an outsider in this small community, so why would this situation be any different? Ten years ago, he'd left Woodmont as a dirt-poor kid determined to be something better than his drunk, verbally abusive father, and today he was a successful multimillionaire and part owner of Premier Realty.

His position within the company wasn't to sell houses and other real estate assets. He bought them. Old, run-down properties and structures that he and one of his partners,

Connor, restored. Once they were finished with the improvements, the realty part of the company resold the place for a hefty profit. In the reality television world, he was labeled a "flipper"—and he fucking hated that term—but his professional business card billed him as a residential and commercial redeveloper.

But what he'd achieved an hour away in Chicago didn't change the way a lot of the townsfolk still viewed him, thanks to his father's belligerent personality and his brother's list of transgressions that had somehow painted him with the same tainted brush and as one of the *no-good Coleman brothers*.

He'd like to believe that time had changed the town's perspective of him, and for the most part, they treated him cordially and civilly, but he'd come to accept that there was one family in particular who would never welcome him with open arms. Yeah, his brother had burned that bridge long ago, and Kyle had been stupid enough to add fuel to the fire that had cost him the girl he'd been crazy in love with. A few unfiltered, hurtful comments spoken in frustration and anger had earned him a sharp slap to the face and a *get out of my life* response that still had the ability to make his stomach clench when he thought about everything he'd lost.

Ella Fisher was, and always would be, the one he'd let slip through his fingers. Obeying those words and walking away from her was his biggest regret, even if he'd told himself, repeatedly, that it was for the best. That a future together would never have worked out for them. Not after what his brother, Todd, had done to Ella's sister. And not when her father had made it more than clear that Kyle wasn't good enough for his daughter.

Over the past ten years, Kyle had come and gone from Woodmont on a regular basis, at least a few times a month, because his mother still lived here, while his townhouse was in Chicago. After his drunk of a father died and Todd ended up in jail on a manslaughter charge, Kyle made sure that his mother was taken care of and that the house his father had let fall apart was completely restored, since his mother refused to move or leave the small town.

But visiting his mother didn't require him to interact with the residents since Patricia Coleman lived on the outskirts, which enabled him to avoid the main part of town and the possibility of running into Ella Fisher. Thanks to his mother's tendency to keep him abreast of everyone's business in town, the last Kyle heard, Ella had been engaged to a guy they'd gone to high school with after dating him for three years—the news of which had induced a gut-punch sensation in the pit of his belly.

Except Ella had never made it to the altar—the wedding had been called off a few months before the big day nearly a year ago. They were no longer a couple, and Kyle hated that a part of him was relieved, even though he knew there was no chance in hell that he and Ella could ever be what they once were. Unfortunately, no other woman had come close to replacing what he'd once felt for the girl he'd left behind.

Despite his mother's updates, it had been a few years since he'd seen Ella in person, but as he drove past the five-and-dime, then the Family Diner, where his mother had worked all his life—and still did, despite him providing her with enough money to retire on—Kyle realized that was all about to change.

"I have to admit I'm a little curious to see how everything plays out today," Nolan said, once again breaking into his thoughts. "Something like this is as exciting as it gets around here, and I'd rather see it happen live and in person than read it on the front page of the weekly gazette tomorrow or hear about it through gossip from one of my clients at the office," he said of the accounting business Nolan had taken over when his father had retired.

Kyle huffed out a laugh and shook his head. "Do you realize how pathetic you sound right now? That something like this is a major enough source of entertainment for you that you actually took the afternoon off from work to watch it all go down?"

"Yeah, I do," Nolan openly admitted, his grin never wavering. "Welcome back to small-town life, my friend. Trust me, this is going to be big news after today."

The last thing Kyle wanted was to be the center of attention. But his reasons for winning the building outweighed the speculation that was bound to circulate once he purchased the property, and gossip was a small price to pay for his mother's happiness. "Yeah, well, maybe you ought to find yourself a girlfriend and settle down so you have something more pleasurable to occupy your free time."

"I'm working on it." Nolan shrugged.

"Yeah?" Kyle raised a brow as he slowed for a stop sign, genuinely surprised that his friend had his eye on someone specific. "You mean you haven't already gone through all the single ladies in town? I didn't think there were that many left to choose from that you haven't already dated."

"Like Ella, who's been single and available the past year since breaking off her engagement to Tucker Barnes?" his friend quipped, his tone sly.

Kyle jerked his gaze to Nolan, hating the way his entire body tensed at the thought of his best friend dating someone who'd been so completely and utterly *his*, which was ridiculous, since it had been nearly ten years since their bitter breakup. It's not as though he had any claim to her *now*.

"Is that who you're interested in?" he asked, his voice gruffer than he'd intended. "Ella?"

"Jesus. No." Nolan shook his head. "I wouldn't do that to you, though I do find it fascinating that you nearly bit my head off right now just because you *thought* I might be interested in her." He smirked. "Still carrying a torch for your high school sweetheart?"

Nolan was clearly ribbing him, and Kyle refused to react in a way that would give his friend any more reason to provoke him. "Not even close. Trust me, that flame was snuffed out a long time ago and we've both moved on."

Kyle had no illusions that, a decade later, they were different people who led completely opposite lives, and he was certain they had nothing left in common with the starry-eyed teenagers they'd once been. Kyle had royally fucked up whatever they'd once shared, and there was no erasing the pain and anger that had driven them apart.

But he'd be lying if he said he didn't regret the abrupt way things had ended between them. Even now, he wished he hadn't left Woodmont, and Ella, without at least apologizing for the hurtful things he'd said. But as the years rolled by, and more time lapsed without seeing her, it had become harder to make that first move and easier to just avoid her when he was visiting his mother.

"So, who's the lucky girl you've set your sights on?" Kyle asked, shifting the conversation back to Nolan.

"Claire Myers."

Kyle groaned out loud. "Ella's best friend?" His tone was incredulous. "Are you serious? You were a bona fide jerk to her in high school and didn't miss an opportunity to tease and torment her because she was taller than most of the guys in our class. Remember when she wore that green dress to school and you called her the Jolly Green Giant? Not cool, man."

Nolan winced at the reminder. "God, I was such an immature asshole back then."

"Yeah, you were," Kyle agreed with a wholehearted chuckle.

While Kyle had been on the varsity wrestling team, which had earned him a scholarship to University of Chicago, Nolan had been the quintessential cocky quarterback who was a total partier and a player—on the field and off. In contrast, Kyle had been more focused on maintaining his grades for college and had been interested in only one girl—Ella. Back then, Nolan had the pick of any girl he'd wanted, and usually had some cute, petite, perky cheerleader at his beck and call. Claire, on the other hand, had been awkward, skinny, and gangly, and was always stumbling over her own two feet because her legs were so long, which made her a target for ridicule.

"I think you were intimidated by Claire's height since she was a few inches taller than you. You did have a bit of a Napoleon complex before your growth spurt your senior year,"

Kyle said, just to bust his friend's chops, which earned him the flip of a middle finger. "After all this time, what put Claire on your radar for someone you'd want to date?"

"A week ago she came into the office to ask me about some tax advice regarding her grandmother's estate, who recently passed," Nolan told him. "She had on this green miniskirt I swear she'd worn to fucking mock me for what I'd said back in high school. I couldn't stop staring at her gorgeous long legs and toned thighs that were distracting as hell and had me entertaining some pretty inappropriate thoughts during our meeting."

The corner of Kyle's mouth quirked with humor. "Karma is a bitch, isn't it?"

"No shit." Nolan rubbed at the back of his neck with his hand. "When Claire stood up to leave, she asked me if I still thought she looked like the Jolly Green Giant or if she'd finally grown into her long legs. She was challenging me, and I have to admit, it was such a goddamn turn-on that I told her I'd have to reserve judgment until after our first date and I had a chance to see if she could walk in heels without tripping over her feet."

"And she actually fell for that line?" Kyle

11

asked in disbelief.

Nolan shrugged, though there was no denying his overly confident expression. "We're having dinner Friday night, so I'd say the answer to that is an unequivocal yes."

Fisher's Grocery—owned by Ella's father, who'd passed the store's responsibilities to his daughter after his stroke—finally came into view. Kyle pulled his truck into the small parking lot. The auction didn't start for another ten minutes, but there was a group of about a dozen townsfolk already gathered in front of the old building next to the family market. The rumble of his engine drew everyone's attention as he parked, then killed the engine. When he got out of the vehicle with Nolan and people started recognizing him as he approached, he heard the low chatter of gossip already starting.

He'd been prepared for the shock and speculation. Nobody but Nolan knew he planned to bid on the building. Not even his own mother was aware of his intentions, because Kyle knew she would have tried to talk him out of what he saw as an investment, as well as the ability to give his hardworking mom the dream she'd always talked about that had been beyond her reach.

That was going to change after today.

As Kyle and Nolan stood in the back of the small crowd and off to the side, Kyle said a polite hello to Tom Elliott, who owned the barbershop on the corner, his well-groomed gray brows pulled together in a perplexed frown. The old man returned the greeting with a low, "Good to see you, son," though it was evident by Tom's confused expression that he was trying to figure out why Kyle was there when he hadn't attended a town function in ten years.

Kyle nodded his head cordially at Jeanette Jones, a teller at the savings and loan, and smiled amicably at the others who were casting surreptitious glances his way as they waited for the public sale to begin. The only one he didn't see in attendance was Ella, but considering Fisher's Grocery was attached to the property for sale, she still had a few minutes left before she needed to arrive. She probably believed she had no competition for the building, therefore there was no reason to show up early to size up her opposition. As for Kyle, as an experienced contractor and someone who purchased a whole lot of foreclosed properties and business-es, he'd done his due diligence and knew exactly what he was up against. Just one other interested party named Ella Fisher.

The thought of seeing her again after so long filled him with a sense of anticipation, and he exhaled a deep breath to try and dispel the jittery sensation in his stomach.

Nolan pushed his hands into the front pockets of his pants as he stared up at the fifteen-thousand-square-foot building in front of them. "I can't believe that this place is finally going to be developed into something other than the eyesore it's been for as long as I've been alive."

Kyle silently agreed. Piedmont, the former owner, had been a hoarder and a hermit and a miser who'd died leaving his only offspring with the small fortune he'd amassed. Now his son, Louis, was in the process of finally liquidating all his father's assets, just to rid himself of the possessions he had no interest in keeping. This building in particular was old and run-down and in need of serious repair after decades of neglect, but Kyle could easily see the potential for what the structure could develop into with a full renovation.

Dan Briggs, the auctioneer in charge of today's sale, arrived and took his place in front of the small crowd. Less than a minute later, Kyle caught sight of Ella walking out of the connecting market, a bright, self-assured smile on her face and a sassy pep to her step, as if this piece of property was already hers and this auction was just a formality. His gut clenched at what he was about to do to her, but he couldn't let himself be deterred by an emotion such as guilt.

Without looking at who was gathered to watch the sale, she walked up to Dan and spoke to him for a few moments, even laughing at something he said, though Kyle couldn't hear their conversation. But he did have a clear view of Ella, and he took advantage of the opportunity to really study her without her guard being up, as he knew it would be as soon as he topped her first bid.

It had been years since the last time he'd seen her. In high school, she'd been a pretty girl, with a lithe body that had tempted him to indulge in all sorts of sin. She'd had a sweet innocence about her that had effortlessly drawn him in. She was still slender with graceful long legs, but her curves were more pronounced and womanly. Her fitted jeans emphasized the alluring dip of her waist along with the tight shape of her spectacular ass. She was wearing a light blue T-shirt with Fisher's Grocery printed across her chest, and it didn't escape Kyle's notice that the breasts that had once been small swells of flesh were now firm and full and would overflow in his big hands in the best possible way.

Her delicate features had matured, but she still possessed that natural beauty that didn't require any cosmetics or enhancements. Judging by the loose braid hanging halfway down her back, she'd let her once-shoulder-length style grow quite a few inches, and he found himself wondering how those chestnut strands would look completely unconfined, and if her hair was still as soft and silky as he remembered.

Something in his belly tightened, and he recognized it as attraction and desire, even after all this time. If Ella were anyone else, or a woman he'd seen at a bar in the city, he would have already been working his way toward her to introduce himself and to see if the chemistry was reciprocated. And from there, he'd buy her a drink, they'd talk a bit, and he'd get a feel for if she was up for a mutual night of pleasure.

Kyle killed that line of thinking. As much as Ella still tempted him, he was pretty certain that she'd knee him in the balls before she'd ever date him again. Especially after she learned he was going to be her new business neighbor.

"It's time to get things started," Dan announced.

Ella took a few steps back to give the man some space to deliver the standard spiel that preceded most real estate auctions. She was so confident that she was the only one interested in the building that she didn't even glance over her shoulder to search the gathering of people behind her.

Dan cleared his throat. "Okay, first let's get all the nitty-gritty details of the auction out of the way. The owner has requested that this be a cash-only sale, and no loans will be accepted. Twenty percent of the winning bid must be paid immediately upon purchase, and the balance must be satisfied in full within twenty-four hours of the sale, or the property is forfeited and another auction will take place. There are no liens on the property, and the building will be sold in an 'as is' condition. Are there any questions before we begin?"

Since all the information for the auction and property had been posted online, Kyle had already done his research on the terms and conditions of the sale and purchase of the property. Here, in a small town where a run-down building wasn't something that normal investors flocked to, the rules were a bit more lax. Still, he'd arrived with a lot of cash in his pocket for the down payment, a notarized statement from the bank certifying the available funds in his personal savings account, and the ability to wire transfer said funds to the seller within a twenty-four-hour period.

When no one spoke up with any inquiries, Dan gave a satisfied nod and began soliciting bids for the property. "Who would like to offer the minimum opening bid of one hundred thousand dollars?" he asked, his gaze on Ella as she immediately raised her hand.

"I will," she said, her energy and enthusiasm nearly tangible as she bounced on the toes of her tennis shoes.

Kyle almost smiled at how adorable she looked, and for a moment even enjoyed the tantalizing jiggle of her breasts as she fidgeted, then quickly remembered that he was about to burst her bubble of excitement and compete with her for the building . . . until he won.

"Is anyone willing to top that bid with an offer of one hundred and twenty-five thousand?" the auctioneer asked, his gaze casually scanning the faces in front of him, as if out of obligation.

Everyone remained quiet, and just as Dan opened his mouth to award Ella the sale, Kyle cut him off. "I'll take that bid," he said, his tone deep, firm, and assertive.

A collective gasp rippled through the crowd, and Ella frowned in confusion as her head jerked in his direction, her eyes searching for the source of the voice that had just thrown her for a loop she hadn't seen coming. A heartbeat later, her lustrous green gaze landed on him, and he watched as her entire body stiffened, her lips parted in shock, and her initial bewilderment transitioned into stunned disbelief.

He inclined his head to acknowledge her, keeping his expression neutral, knowing she was trying to figure out what he was doing there after all this time and why he was competing for the building she wanted. Anger flickered in her eyes, and Kyle was pretty sure if they didn't have an audience, she would have confronted him. Instead, she turned back to Dan and lifted her chin with a conviction he found incredibly sexy.

"One hundred and fifty thousand," she said, upping her bid without the auctioneer even asking.

Kyle crossed his arms over his chest, ignoring the whispers going on around him. "One hundred and seventy-five thousand."

Again, Ella glanced at him, this time incredulously, and he kept his poker face in place. This was where it would get interesting. He had no idea how much cash Ella had secured for the auction, but he doubted that it was anywhere near what he had available within twenty-four hours. How high could she go before she conceded defeat?

She glared at him, her complexion turning pink with frustration. "Two hundred thousand dollars," she announced in a tight voice, glaring at him.

"Two hundred twenty-five thousand," he responded without hesitating. It was more than the building was worth in its present condition considering the improvements it needed, but this purchase wasn't about the money for him, and he had to remind himself of that as he watched Ella's devastated expression declare him as the winner even before the auctioneer did.

God, he felt like the biggest asshole on the planet. By giving one woman her dream, he'd just crushed it for another.

"We have an offer of two hundred and twenty-five thousand dollars," Dan said, looking away from Ella as if he already knew her maximum budget had just been exceeded. "Is anyone willing to top that bid?"

After a few seconds of absolute silence, Ella shook her head. Then, as if she couldn't bear to see the building being awarded to Kyle, she turned around and headed toward the market and disappeared inside. He thought about going after Ella to explain his reasons for wanting the property—not that he'd expect that to soothe her anger and upset—but a couple of the women standing nearby broke away to follow Ella to help ease the blow she'd just been delivered. And Kyle knew he'd be less than welcome anywhere near her.

"Going once . . . going twice . . . *sold* to the gentleman in the black shirt standing in the back row!" the auctioneer finally said, forcing Kyle to draw his gaze away from the grocery store, where Ella had escaped to.

Fuck, he thought as he scrubbed a hand along the short-cropped beard covering his jaw.

He should have been elated to have what he'd wanted for years, to be able to give his mother something just for herself, but he felt like shit instead.

Well, what had he expected? He'd known going in he was going to crush Ella's hopes and dreams. And he didn't feel at all good about himself now that he had.

Chapter Two

UNABLE TO SLEEP, Ella stared wide-eyed at the ceiling of her bedroom, watching the shadows on the walls shift from the gray of night to the first light of dawn as the morning sun started to rise on a brand-new day. A day she'd imagined would be much different and more exciting than the one she was about to face now that her plans for the adjoining building to her father's market had come crashing down around her in the form of Kyle Coleman . . . the first guy she'd ever loved and had never truly gotten over, despite the way things had ended between them.

She was still in a state of disbelief at seeing him after so many years, not to mention feeling like a fool for thinking that no one else wanted the old, decrepit building. She'd actually thought her bid was just a technicality to ensure that the property was hers. Absolutely *nothing* had prepared her for losing the one thing she'd had her sights set on for the past five years so she could finally expand Fisher's Grocery into something more. And she certainly hadn't been braced to see the gorgeous man who still had the ability to make her feel breathless and weak-kneed when she should have gotten over him a long time ago.

She released a loud growl of frustration as she punched the pillow next to her, grateful that her father slept on the opposite side of the house so she didn't wake him up with all her tossing and turning and cursing during the course of the night. She'd already been bombarded with angry questions from her only parent that she hadn't been able to answer as soon as she'd gotten home last night after closing the market. *What did Kyle want with the building? Had he purchased the place out of spite so Ella couldn't claim it? Why after all these years would he want anything that tied him to Woodmont when he lived his life in Chicago?*

Ella honestly didn't know, but she wondered all those things, too. She'd heard that he'd become one of those guys who bought old houses and buildings and renovated them to resell, but anyone who lived in Woodmont knew there weren't any big profits to be had in redeveloping commercial property here. Not like there was in the city, where real estate was at a premium. The town was small, the residents set in their ways, and what else did they need that other businesses didn't already provide?

Everything about Kyle's interest in Piedmont's building was a mystery, and her emotions were still running the gamut from the elation she was so sure she'd feel to the depths of confusion and anger she'd plummeted to. The shock of everything was starting to wear off and and reality was beginning to sink in, but there was no denying that she was now overwhelmed with resentment . . . and ashamed to admit that she was too damn aware of all the changes in Kyle, who'd grown from the cute, boyish teenager she'd been so smitten with despite her father's warning to stay away from him, to the impressive man he was now with a presence that was commanding and confident.

A decade later, and Kyle was utterly dropdead gorgeous, his features more masculine and mature and handsome. She even begrudgingly admitted that the neatly trimmed beard on his face added to his rugged appeal, and for a moment she pondered what it might feel like against her fingertips . . . or skimming along her thighs. Course and bristly or soft and ticklish?

Shifting restlessly beneath the sheets, she groaned and closed her eyes, unable to stop herself from conjuring the image of him standing there yesterday in his tight black T-shirt stretching across his broad shoulders and wide chest, with his tanned arms folded in front of him, biceps flexing and bad-boy tattoos on display, and looking *so freaking hot*. Everything about him intrigued her, and just thinking about him now elicited a tingling warmth of awareness to course through her veins.

And yeah, the fact that Kyle Coleman still had that kind of sensual effect on any part of her body pissed Ella off even more than she already was.

Her alarm went off right on time at five a.m., and she reached over to her nightstand to shut it off instead of hitting the snooze button a few times like she normally did. This morning, she wanted to be out the door before her father woke up to avoid another interrogation about Kyle when she had no answers that would satisfy her dad. The last thing she needed was him getting worked up again and raising his blood pressure or worse. He already blamed one Coleman brother for the stroke he'd had that had left him with permanent nerve damage that had also affected his fine motor skills, and she didn't need Kyle's actions yesterday to be the cause of something equally tragic. Even if inadvertently.

She forced herself up and into the shower and was out of the house within a half hour, secure in the knowledge that Betsy, the woman who helped take care of her father and the house during the day, would be there in an hour to start breakfast for her dad, even before he had a chance to wake up.

Ella made it to the market before the first scheduled delivery of the morning arrived at six a.m., and for the next hour, her mind was occupied with signing for the steady stream of daily perishables the store had on a standing order. By seven, Fisher's Grocery's longtime manager, William, showed up, as well as half a dozen other employees who were scheduled to work their shifts for the day. With William now in charge, she headed into the office at the back of the store and closed herself inside. She had some difficult phone calls to make, to people she'd made promises to . . . when she'd been so certain the adjoining building would belong to her.

One by one, she made her way through the list of local artisans she'd discussed consignment arrangements with for their various products, to let them know that the expansion would not be happening and she had no room in the actual market to carry their merchandise. Their disappointment was as keen as her own. By the time she was done with the painful calls, she was frustrated all over again that Kyle had stolen something that would have been hers and hers alone.

Not her family's. Not her father's. *Hers.*

Beyond miffed, she made an unhappy sound and tossed her pencil onto her desktop just as Claire, her best friend and bookkeeper for Fisher's Grocery, walked into the office wearing a white eyelet blouse, pink capris, and a pair of flats, her blonde hair perfectly styled in a silky chin-length bob that looked fabulous on her. As always, she looked fresh and pretty compared to Ella's normal jeans-and-T-shirt attire that usually ended up dirty from manual labor by the end of the day.

Her friend raised a brow at Ella's sullen expression as she hung her purse from a hook on the wall, then settled into a chair in front of the desk. She crossed one long leg over the other, and just like any good friend would do, she didn't sugarcoat her next comment.

"Sorry to have to tell you this, but you look like hell."

"I *feel* like hell," Ella said as she pressed the tips of her fingers against her temple, where a nagging headache had been pestering her all morning. "I barely slept last night, and on top of that, I feel like an ass for making promises to so many businesses that I had to turn around and break."

Her idea to expand her family's store to include more handcrafted items from local vendors—such as organic cheeses, breads, seasonings, and even maple syrups and jams and jellies—had been well received by the town, and she loved the thought of supporting local artisans in the community. Her concept had been a daily farmer's-market-type offering of goods that were gourmet and unique and would give shoppers the opportunity to purchase specialty items all in one place, rather than having to travel thirty miles or more to a big-box store. And as large as the building next door was, it would have given the market itself room to grow, as well.

So much for any of that.

"I'm really sorry," Claire said, her tone sincere. "I know losing the building is tough on you, but you have to know it's not your fault."

She appreciated her friend's sympathetic words, but they didn't make her feel any better. "Maybe it *is* my fault," Ella said, expressing the fact that she'd been second-guessing herself all night. "Maybe I should have been more prepared for someone else to bid on the building. At least have taken out a larger loan to have more money in reserve, just in case." God, hindsight was such a bitch.

"Who would even want to own that ugly building?" Claire said with a small laugh. "I mean, other than you, of course."

"That's exactly what I thought, and look where that got me. Absolutely nowhere." She opened a side drawer and withdrew the bottle of ibuprofen she kept stashed there and tapped a few of the tablets into her palm. "What could Kyle possibly want with the building when he hasn't lived here for the past ten years? It's hardly the kind of investment any shrewd or savvy developer would be interested in." She tossed back the headache medicine, washed the pills down with water, and prayed for relief, and soon.

"Now that's the two-hundred-and-twenty-five-thousand-dollar question, isn't it?" Claire drummed her pink-painted fingernails on the arm of the chair, her expression thoughtful. "Bottom line, you want answers, and there's only one person who can give them to you. So why don't you go and get them?"

Ella frowned at her friend. "What do you mean?"

"Go right to the source," Claire said with a shrug. "In this case, that would be Kyle."

Go and confront Kyle? Claire's idea was insane, and Ella quickly shook her head. "I don't know how to get ahold of him. Where he lives or even the name of his company."

A slow, mischievous smile curved the corners of Claire's lips, making Ella immediately wary. "Well, you could head over to the Family Diner and ask his mother those questions, but since I know you'd never do that, let's see what good ol' Google has to say about a Kyle Coleman who lives and works in Chicago."

Before Ella realized what her friend meant

to do, Claire leaned across the desk and grabbed her cell phone. Ella quickly scrambled to retrieve it, but Claire sat back in her chair, out of arm's reach.

"Hey, give me my phone back," Ella demanded.

"In a sec." Claire's fingers tapped across the keyboard on the screen, and a moment later she glanced up at Ella with a triumphant grin. "Well, would you look at this," she said in an irritatingly sweet drawl as she read the information she'd found. "Kyle Coleman. Redeveloper at Premier Realty. And there's a phone number and a street address to his office." She batted her lashes in feigned shock. "Who would have thought that he'd be listed on the Internet and so easy to find in this day and age?"

"You're such a smartass," Ella grumbled, though she was smiling.

"It's why you love me." Claire's green eyes sparkled with humor. "You work too hard, you're way too serious, and I keep things lively around here."

"Yeah, okay, whatever."

Ella rolled her eyes, but the truth was, if it wasn't for Claire, she'd probably have no real after-hours social life, and she wouldn't laugh nearly as much as she did when she was around her best friend. Yes, she worked ten- to twelve-hour days and rarely took time off, and that's pretty much how it had been since she'd taken on the responsibility of managing the market after her father's stroke ten years ago. It had been the right thing to do because of his limitations, even if it had meant giving up her plans to go to college.

Between her and her self-centered, flighty sister, Gwen, Ella had always been the dependable one in the family, despite the fact that they were "Irish twins," with Gwen being older by only ten months. Ella was the one who never colored outside the lines and always stepped up to take care of everyone else's needs before her own. After their mother had passed away, she'd been the one to take on the task of cooking dinner every night, even though she'd only been thirteen at the time. She'd made sure her father's clothes were laundered, that the house was picked up, and *tried* to keep her sister out of trouble so their father didn't have to deal with Gwen's numerous acts of teenage rebellion.

So yes, Ella had been the quintessential good girl—the one caveat to that being going against her father's demand to stay away from Kyle Coleman during her senior year in high school. And in the end, what did she get for her one act of defiance? She'd been left with a shattered heart and her family's life in an emotional upheaval. Although the upheaval had been more the fault of Gwen's actions than her own, Ella had been left to deal with the fallout.

"Holy smokes," Claire said in awe as she turned her phone toward Ella to show her the photo she'd found on the Premier Realty website. "Damn, Kyle Coleman is *gorgeous*. And hot. And built like a brick house, compared to how lean he was in high school."

Ella wasn't about to admit that she'd already spent part of last night obsessing over that good-looking face, those dark brown eyes, and the impressive muscles he'd developed over the years.

Claire swiped a few things on the face of the phone before giving it back to Ella. The photo was gone, and now on display was the address and phone number of Premier Realty highlighted for her to see.

She chewed her lower lip uncertainly before she met her friend's gaze from across the desk. "So, you think I should call him?"

"No. That's too easy and not bold enough," Claire said, waving a dismissive hand in the air. "I think you should go to his office and look him in the eye when you ask him what you want to know. Maybe you could even offer him a bit more for the building to buy it from him. You didn't have the cash on hand yesterday, but you know you could get a bank loan for the difference."

The store's credit was solid, their bills paid in full every month, and she was certain that she could get an increase on their line of credit for the investment back into the business. She definitely wanted the building that much, but what if she went to Kyle and he refused any offer she made? He'd outbid her yesterday without flinching at the cost, so what made her think he'd give up the property so easily now?

"I don't know," she said, hating the defeated way she sounded.

"That's just it. You *don't* know until you try," Claire refuted in that confident, reasonable way of hers. "What if he's willing to take a bit of a profit, hand over the building, and walk away? You'll never know unless you make the offer, and if you don't do this, you'll always wonder what if."

Claire's advice, as always, was sound and logical. "Okay," she agreed, but only to part of her friend's suggestion. "I'll *call* him." It was a compromise.

Claire narrowed her gaze. "No calling. You need to do this in person, face-to-face. The element of surprise will throw him off-balance, just like he did to you yesterday. That could work in your favor."

It was hard for Ella to imagine that anything would throw Kyle off his game, but there was another more important reason she hesitated to jump on Claire's idea. "You know I *hate* going into the city." Actually, hate was a mild word for how she felt about Chicago. *Loathed* was more like it.

Chicago was only an hour's drive away, without any traffic, but the half dozen or so times that she'd gone into the city, she'd nearly had a legitimate anxiety attack. There were too many people around and all in one place, and the blend of sirens wailing, vehicles honking, and subways rumbling beneath her feet had been sensory overload when she was so used to her peaceful small town. Everything was too fast-paced, too overpopulated, and she'd been overwhelmed by all the tall buildings surrounding her. She always felt too closed in, like a panicked mouse in a maze with no way out.

The last time she'd been to Chicago had been a year ago with her fiancé, Tucker—an evening she'd agreed to because she'd hoped the different environment might make her see him in a new light. That maybe, hopefully, being somewhere with him that he'd deemed as romantic would spark some kind of real passion between them.

Instead, going into the city had made her realize two important things. One, she never wanted to go back if she could help it. And two, once she was sitting across from Tucker at the five-star restaurant where he'd made reservations for what should have been a seductive and amorous evening, she'd come to the difficult and painful realization that it could never work between them. Her phobia of the city and her breakup with Tucker soon after that had nothing to do with each other, but neither had been pleasant experiences she ever wanted to go through again.

"Don't you think this is one trip that might be worth making?" Claire asked, cutting into her thoughts. Her tone was both understanding of Ella's aversion to the city and a bit of tough love, too. "You can't let that building go without some kind of fight. You've been planning the expansion for years, just waiting for Old Man Piedmont to pass on so his son could finally sell the place. Don't you want to know that you did everything in your power to try and get the building, instead of wondering if you could have done more?"

God, why did Claire have to be so smart and truthful? And damn pushy, she tacked on for good measure. The last thing Ella wanted to carry around for the next thirty years was the regret of not knowing if the building could have been hers.

She exhaled a deep breath. "You're right," she muttered.

"Of course I am." Claire flashed her a victorious smile. "So you need to do it. Today. Before too much time passes and you chicken out."

"Okay, okay! Jesus, you're one persistent broad," Ella said with a laugh as she stood up. "I might as well go and get it over with."

Claire wrinkled her nose as she visually appraised Ella's faded jeans and old T-shirt attire. "Umm, you're not going like *that*, are you?"

Seriously? "What's wrong with how I look?"

"Did we not just establish that you look like hell?" Claire made an unappealing face. "You need to go home and do something with your hair instead of wearing it in that stuffy braid that makes you look like a spinster, and change into something that shows a little leg and cleavage."

Ella gaped at her friend. What did it matter how she looked? "I'm not going there to seduce him, for crying out loud." Besides, as gorgeous and citified as Kyle looked, she was sure he had a girlfriend, or at least a dozen beautiful women at his beck and call who captivated him better than she ever could.

"Not to *seduce* him," Claire retorted with a devious smile. "To *distract* him."

Ella braced her hands on her desk and raised a knowing brow at her friend. "Oh, kind of like how you wore that short skirt to your meeting with Nolan about your grandmother's estate?"

"Oh, that wasn't to distract him," she replied slyly. "It was to prove a point, that these long legs have nothing to do with the Jolly Green Giant. And it worked, didn't it? Which proves I'm right. Dress for success."

"Considering how Nolan tormented you in

high school, I can't believe you're going on a date with him."

"Hey, it's getting to be slim pickings around here," Claire said, which was sadly true when it came to the selection of single men left to choose from in Woodmont. "Besides, he's grown up, like we all have, and he's not the jerk that he once was. Even if we just go out and have a good time and it leads to a hot and heavy hookup, I'm not about to complain. It's been too freaking long since I've had an orgasm that wasn't induced by my battery-operated boyfriend. There's something to be said for getting fucked by real fingers, an agile tongue, and a true-to-life dick."

Ella burst out laughing and shook her head, but she wholeheartedly agreed with her friend. "Yeah, I hear you." It had been a year since her breakup with Tucker, and even when they'd been together, he hadn't been overtly sexual, which had been part of the issue between them. Sure, sweet and kind and attentive were great attributes when it came to a man, but sometimes, a girl just wanted to be fucked hard and mindlessly . . . and not always in the same old missionary position. Her own vibrator had been more creative than Tucker ever had been, and always guaranteed an orgasm.

"You'll hold down the fort for a few hours while I'm gone?" Ella asked Claire as she grabbed her purse from the hook on the wall.

"This place isn't going anywhere, and we'll survive a few hours without you." Claire stood up and gave her a shooing motion with her hands. "Now go already."

Ella headed for the door, thinking about what she could wear for her meeting with Kyle that was appropriate, then came to an abrupt stop. "Oh, crap, I can't go home and change." She turned around to face Claire again. "My father will know something's up and he'll bombard me with questions. I don't want him to know that I'm going to talk to Kyle, either, because he'll have a heart attack." She winced when she realized what she'd just insinuated, considering her father had already had a stroke because of one Coleman brother's actions.

"Yeah, bad choice of words," Claire needlessly pointed out, the corner of her mouth kicking up in humor. "Go to my place instead. I'm sure you can find a skirt and blouse that will work. And our shoe size is the same. It's not like you haven't worn my clothes before."

Ella exhaled a relieved breath. "True, and

thank you."

With luck, she'd be in and out of the city in no time, and once Kyle heard her reasons for wanting the building, he'd hopefully agree to sell it to her.

A girl could dream, couldn't she?

✦   ✦   ✦

ELLA DIDN'T INTEND on driving into the city at three in the freaking afternoon, but just when she'd been about to leave the market to go and change at Claire's, her manager, William, stopped her before she'd made it out to her car to let her know he'd just discovered a coolant leak in the refrigeration system. The temperatures in the coolers were steadily increasing, putting their dairy products and perishables at risk.

Their normal maintenance guy had arrived at the store a half an hour later and assured Ella the leak wasn't a major repair and would only take a few hours. Could she have left William to handle the crisis? Probably, but considering the potential liability of losing thousands of dollars in food, she hadn't been able to bring herself to go until she knew for certain everything was back up in working order. Which meant by the time she changed at Claire's and hit the road, it was much later in the afternoon before she arrived in Chicago, instead of the earlier morning visit she'd anticipated.

While Ella had been talking to the technician about the cost of repair and what was required, Claire had taken it upon herself to call Premier Realty to inquire whether or not Kyle would be in the office so Ella didn't make a wasted trip. The receptionist told her that Kyle would be in until six, and before the girl could ask her name, Claire said a quick good-bye and hung up the phone. She'd gotten the information she needed and happily passed it on to Ella—and she was grateful that her friend had thought ahead for her. The last thing she wanted to do was make the trek only to find out that Kyle wasn't in for her to see.

Getting from Woodmont to Chicago hadn't been too bad on the interstate, but now that she was navigating the inner city at five p.m., when rush hour was at its heaviest and everyone was eager to get home—not to mention a Friday night and the start to the weekend—the cluster of cars in such a close proximity had Ella's entire body tense as she followed the directions she'd pulled up on Google Maps. The robotic female voice instructed her to make a left at the next light, and Ella must not have done it quickly enough for the person behind her, who laid on the horn, which in turn made her panic and cut in front of another vehicle, whose driver rightly flipped her off for the stupid move, because, yeah, she'd been *that* asshole who had nearly caused an accident.

Jesus Christ. Her heart was pounding and her palms were sweaty against the steering wheel by the time she finally made it to Kyle's office building. Nerves frazzled, she turned into the underground parking structure that immediately made her feel claustrophobic, and pulled a ticket from the machine, which then allowed the lever to rise so she could drive into the confined space. Since it was after five, she easily found a spot, and as soon as she was parked, she killed the engine, unbuckled her seat belt, and gave herself five minutes to decompress and collect her composure before she had to face her nemesis.

When she finally felt like she wasn't going to jump out of her skin, and her heart rate was back to normal, she got out of the car. She smoothed a hand down the skirt she'd confiscated from Claire's closet as she headed for the bank of elevators, more than satisfied with her choice of outfit.

When she'd arrived at Claire's house earlier and she'd looked through all her cute clothes, Ella came to the spontaneous decision that she wanted to look not just good for this meeting but *exceptionally* good—to show Kyle that she might be a small-town girl, but she could be just as sophisticated and sexy as any other woman in the city.

Yesterday, he'd seen her in faded jeans and a T-shirt that had to be at least five years old. Today, she intended to look like a confident woman in charge, and per Claire's suggestion, she'd opted for a bit of cleavage, a flirty skirt, and heeled platform pumps that showed off her legs. Kyle was a man, after all, and she figured a little physical distraction wouldn't hurt her cause.

She pressed the button for the elevator and actually smiled. *Let the negotiations begin.*

Chapter Three

THE QUICK RAPPING sound on the doorframe of his office prompted Kyle to glance up from the renovation estimate he'd been working on for one of the new foreclosed homes Premier Reality had just purchased in the high-end neighborhood of Wicker Park. They still had a few weeks before the project started, but they needed to get the agreements for subcontractors underway before the redevelopment of the property began.

Connor Prescott, one of Kyle's business partners and good friends, strolled into the office, the dust on his jeans and work boots the result of a day spent out on various property sites that were currently being updated and/or overhauled for a more modern look before they were put back on the market. Kyle was usually out in the field, as well, but since he'd needed to be in the office to make sure the wire transfer and all the paperwork and contracts for the Piedmont building went through smoothly, he'd spent the day getting ahead on the estimates for the future projects coming down the pipeline.

"So, I hear congratulations are in order," Connor said as he gave Kyle a smartass look. "You're now the proud owner of a run-down, dilapidated building in a Podunk town. I hope the eventual return is worth the investment."

Kyle leaned back in his chair, refusing to let his friend goad him or dampen his good mood. The property in Woodmont wasn't about the monetary return or even a revenue stream for Kyle, because clearly he wasn't going to make bank on his purchase when it had cost him nearly double what the building was worth. It was about giving his hardworking mother the one thing she'd always wistfully talked about but never believed could become a reality. Kyle truly didn't give a shit if he didn't make a penny on the purchase. He just wanted his mom to be happy and to be able to spend the rest of her years doing what she loved.

Buying the building had been a complete

surprise for his mother, and when he'd driven to her house after the auction to tell her that the property was now his and what he planned to do with it, he knew he'd made the right decision when he'd seen how unbelievably overjoyed she'd been . . . as long as he didn't think about Ella's devastated expression after he'd been awarded the property.

Kyle returned his attention to Connor and smirked as he rubbed his palm against his bearded jaw. "Just so you know, starting next Saturday, you'll be volunteering your weekends to help me gut the place before the renovations start." They had about a month before all the licenses and permits for the place were approved, but in the meantime, clearing out Piedmont's years of hoarded crap was a priority.

"Yeah, I figured," Connor said with a good-natured shake of his head. "Seriously, though, I'm happy for you, and whatever you need, I'm there for you."

"Thanks, man. I appreciate it." It went without saying that Kyle could always count on Connor, and the other two guys he worked with, for anything.

Connor rubbed his hands together. "So, what do you say we blow this joint and I buy you a beer to celebrate your new venture?"

Kyle laughed. "If you're buying, then hell yeah."

He pushed his chair back and stood up just as the intercom on his desk beeped and the receptionist's voice came through. "Kyle, I have an Ella Fisher here to see you," Daphne informed him. "She said she doesn't have an appointment. Do you have time to meet with her, or should I schedule her for another day since it's after five?"

"I just spent over two hours on the road and I'd really like to see him today, if possible," Kyle heard Ella say to Daphne in the background, her tone almost desperate. And annoyed.

"Holy shit," Kyle muttered beneath his breath. Ella was *here?* He was so shocked by her impromptu visit that it took a few extra seconds for him to wrap his brain around that fact.

"Kyle?" Daphne asked, clearly waiting for his answer.

"No, it's fine," he replied, his curiosity getting the best of him. That and it would be a total dick move to make Ella schedule an appointment for another day after driving from Woodmont, and being that kind of dick wasn't his style. "I'll see Ms. Fisher. Show her back to my office, please."

The line disconnected. Kyle was dying to know what had prompted Ella to seek him out, though he'd bet money it had something to do with the building he'd bought. As much as he'd like to wish her reasons for this visit were more personal, he knew she wasn't there to make up for lost time between them. No, any chance of a reconciliation had been diminished years ago.

Kyle glanced up at his friend with an apologetic look. "I'm going to have to take a rain check on that beer."

Conner tipped his head speculatively. "Ms. Fisher must be someone pretty important."

"She's the woman I told you about. The one I bought the Piedmont building out from under," Kyle said, rounding his desk before she arrived. "She had no idea anyone else was bidding on the property, so she was a little . . . blindsided."

Connor's eyes widened comically. "Oh, Jesus. So, in other words, you're dealing with a woman scorned. I'm outta here."

Kyle chuckled at Connor's quick decision to avoid getting caught in the middle of any potential conflict between himself and Ella.

"Chickenshit," he teased his friend.

Connor took no offense and grinned. "I don't do drama, so whatever it is between you and this girl, you're on your own."

His friend headed for the door just as the receptionist appeared with Ella right behind her, forcing Connor to abruptly stop or run into the two women. Not bothering to wait for introductions, Connor gave Ella a curt nod, then beelined it down the hall.

"Here you go, Ms. Fisher," Daphne said, sweeping a hand through the doorframe. As soon as Ella walked inside the office, the young girl glanced at him and said, "Would you like the door left open or closed?"

Kyle casually leaned his backside against the desk behind him. Most everyone was gone for the evening, but the last thing he wanted right now was any kind of interruption. "Closed, please."

The girl did as he asked, and then he was completely alone with Ella for the first time in ten long years. She stopped a good five feet away from him, and the silence in the room was absolute as she quickly glanced around his office while he drank in the sight of her.

Yesterday had been all about business, but

as he looked at her right now, all he could think of was *pleasure* and how much he still wanted and desired her on a gut-deep level—despite all the past hurt and pain still lingering between them. Not to mention any anger she might be harboring after losing the Piedmont building to him. It was hard to believe she *still* had that kind of intense effect on him when no other woman had ever come close to making him feel—*and want*—like she did.

At the auction the day before, in her T-shirt and jeans and hair pulled back into a loose braid, she'd been the pretty, wholesome girl—who'd grown into a woman's body—he remembered from high school. Today, she'd transformed into stunningly beautiful. She'd obviously put on just enough makeup to accentuate her light green eyes and long lashes, and the pale peach gloss on her lips drew his gaze to her lush mouth before he moved on to the gorgeous chestnut hair falling in soft waves around her shoulders and down her back. The overhead lighting caught on the natural red and gold undertones threading through the strands and made his fingers itch to touch.

If she'd meant to tease him with that short, flirty pale yellow skirt that skimmed a few inches above the knee and the white blouse that was buttoned low enough for him to glimpse a bit of cleavage and lace beneath—not to mention those heels that made her legs look endlessly long and prompted some indecent thoughts that would undoubtedly make her blush—then she'd succeeded. Why else would she wear something so fucking sexy, if not to addle his mind and divert his focus?

By the time he lifted his gaze back to her face, certain parts of his anatomy definitely felt heated and restless, but his concentration was just fine. It was a damn good thing he was an excellent multitasker, because he wasn't done enjoying the enticing view she presented, and he was certain she wasn't here for a social call. Balancing the two was no problem for him.

He gripped his fingers around the edge of the desk he was leaning against as they stared at each other for a long moment. Her gaze was guarded, her body language surprisingly composed despite the uneasy way she bit on that bottom lip of hers—which only served to remind him of how soft and pliant her sweet mouth used to feel beneath his.

"It's good to see you, Ella," he said, finally breaking the silence between them, though the raspy tone of his voice betrayed his casual air.

"You, too," she replied automatically.

A half smile twitched at the corner of his mouth. He wasn't quite sure he believed her. He doubted that she honestly felt it was good to see him, when she looked like she'd rather be anywhere but in the same space with him. He hated her polite reserve, her feigned indifference, and decided to use a little humor to cut through the tension a bit—because being on the receiving end of that cool facade of hers sucked.

"So, what brings you to Premier Realty?" he asked amicably, as if she were a friend instead of a foe. "Looking for a place in the city?"

She visibly shuddered. "God, no." Her aversion to Chicago came through loud and clear in the distasteful tone of her voice. Then, in a more no-nonsense and direct manner, she lifted her chin and said, "You know why I'm here, Kyle."

Ahhh, fuck. Just the sound of his name on her lips was enough to bring him to his knees. "I can't say I do," he fibbed as he continued to tease her, attempting to draw out a smile or, at the very least, see her relax with him. "I mean, you look like you're dressed for a Friday night in the city. Or maybe you just dropped by to say

hi to your new business neighbor, since we'll be
seeing a lot of each other over the next month
or two?"

Her full, shiny lips pursed tightly in exasper-
ation—not the reaction he'd been aiming for.
"No, I came to make an offer to my hopefully
soon-to-be *ex*-business neighbor."

Ouch. The emphasis on the word *ex* was especially painful for many reasons, but he wasn't
dissuaded. Yet. "So, you came by to proposition
me?" he asked in a flirtatious tone.

"Yes . . . *no*," she quickly amended when she
realized what she'd agreed to. She looked
thoroughly flustered, her complexion blushing
an attractive shade of pink. "Not like that."

He shrugged and shoved the tips of his fingers into the front pockets of his jeans. "Can't
blame a guy for trying."

She frowned at him. So much for coaxing a
smile from her or breaking the ice.

She released a slow breath, and the rigid set
of her shoulders slackened a bit as she met his
gaze, her own imploring. "Kyle . . . I want that
building. Badly," she said in a soft voice that
lacked any of the frustration or the attitude that
had accompanied her into his office a few
moments ago. "I'd planned on expanding the

market, which is long overdue, and I already had local artisans lined up to sell their products in the addition, as well."

She shifted on her heels and swallowed hard, and he knew this plea wasn't easy for her. "I don't know why you bought the building in the first place when you don't even live in Woodmont, but I'd like you to sell it to me. I'm willing to offer what you paid for it, plus an additional ten percent on top of that for your trouble. It's not a bad profit for one day's time."

His stomach twisted into a giant knot of re-gret, because at the moment, with her guard down, she looked so relatable. And so much more vulnerable, which added to the emotional conflict he was suddenly experiencing. His Ella had always been feisty and strong-willed, and he could only imagine what it had taken for her to show him anything less than confidence and unwavering determination. She was such a fighter, and he was about to crush any chance she believed she might have to get the building back.

"I'm sorry, Ella. It's not for sale. At any price." His tone was gentle but firm. There was no room for negotiation on this issue for him.

A fine sheen of moisture glistened in her

green eyes, and he suspected the tears she was valiantly holding back were out of sheer disappointment. "Are you doing this to spite me or because of some kind of grudge you're holding against me or my family from the past?" she asked, her voice hoarse.

"*What?*" Her question momentarily took him aback. "Jesus, *no.*"

He pushed his fingers through his hair, hating that she believed such a thing, that she believed, even a little bit, that he'd had malicious intentions. God, their past was so complicated, not to mention all the bitter, angry emotions still lingering between them. So many awful things said in the heat of the moment that had never been fixed or explained or apologized for, and had been kept alive for ten long years.

Driven purely by instinct, he pushed away from the desk and slowly approached Ella until he'd closed the distance between them. She tipped her head back slightly to look up at him, more than a little wary, though she didn't move away. Her eyes were wide and luminous and revealed just enough pain—the emotional kind that was equivalent to a knife twisting in his chest—and he wanted it gone. All of it. The hurt, the animosity, the resentment . . . *everything.*

He wanted a clean slate between them.

They'd never be what they once were—young and in love and hopeful about a future together—but he'd like to believe that they might be able to at least be friends going forward. But even that couldn't happen until he made amends for his past mistakes.

Without thinking through his actions, he lifted a hand and brushed a soft strand of hair away from the side of her face. His fingers skimmed along her cheek, and she sucked in a startled breath, not in fear or panic but in undeniable awareness of his touch. It wasn't wishful thinking, either. It was a fact, because her beautiful, expressive eyes truly were, and had always been, windows to her soul. Even after all this time, he recognized the subtle longing and undisguised desire before she realized what she'd revealed with that small sound and those irresistible green irises. Seconds later, she seemed to regain her presence of mind and moved her head back, severing the connection between them.

Kyle dropped his hand back to his side. "Ella . . . there is no spite as far as I'm concerned, and I've *never* held a grudge," he told her truthfully. He wasn't sure if this was the time or the place, but if he didn't finally say the words that he'd kept to himself for too long, he feared he'd lose the opportunity. "I know this is coming ten years too late, but I'm so sorry about what happened that night, for the things I said and how it all ended. For your sister . . ." *a shocking miscarriage.* "For your father . . ." *a debilitating stroke.* "For us . . . " *accusations, outrage, and a bitter breakup that had cost him the best thing in his life.* Her.

He exhaled a deep breath, and holding her gaze, he finished. "Walking away from you was the most difficult thing I've ever done, and the second most difficult thing was not going back to Woodmont to make things right. I never should have left despite you wanting me gone. I should have been there for you when you needed someone the most."

Her eyes widened as she stared at him in shock, clearly stunned by his admission, though he did notice that her defensive posture eased. He didn't want or expect a reciprocating response or even her acknowledgement of any regrets she might have had after all this time. That's not why he'd apologized. He just wanted to make amends, and he needed Ella to know how sorry he was. They were both adults now, and holding on to any kind of resentment was petty and ridiculous.

When she didn't respond, he continued. "My reasons for buying the building have nothing to do with you or your family. My reasons are personal. I've been waiting for years for that property to go on sale so I could purchase it."

"So have I," she said quietly, though her brows furrowed just a fraction, her expression perplexed. "Why do you want it?"

"It's for my mother."

"Your mother?" Her tone was laced with confusion. "What does Patricia want with the building?"

"It's what *I* want for her," he corrected—and had since he was a young boy. From a very young age, he remembered many times when he and his mother had walked by the Piedmont building with him holding her hand, and how she'd wistfully tell him that she'd love to own that storefront. She imagined turning it into a beautiful event center that also did catering, along with an attached bakery so she could do the one thing she loved the most.

Instead, she'd spent the ensuing years baking at home and taking her goods to the Family

Diner, where she worked as a waitress, and the owners of the restaurant purchased her cakes, pies, and desserts to sell to their customers. It had been her way to make extra money to make ends meet, since Kyle's father had spent most of his paycheck on alcohol. But baking was also her joy and passion, and her dream was the one thing he could give her.

"I'll be turning the place into an event center for different occasions, like holiday and retirement parties, award banquets, weddings, and those sorts of things." And his mother would have her bakery, as well.

She shook her head, causing her silky hair to shift across her shoulders. "That's what the community center and church hall are for."

He arched a pointed brow. "Sure, if you like the smell of mothballs and damp, musty rooms. Both places and all the facilities for catering are old, run-down, and extremely outdated."

She didn't argue with that, but she did try a different approach. "I can't imagine that there will be enough events within a month's time to make buying and renovating the building worthwhile."

"Maybe, maybe not." He shrugged. "But it's not about the money, Ella. It's about seeing my mother happy and not strapped to a nine-to-five waitressing job for the rest of her life." Though working at the Family Diner was now his mother's choice, considering the amount of money he'd deposited into her personal savings account, which she refused to touch. Stubborn woman. "It's what she deserves after sacrificing so much to take care of everyone else for most of her life."

Ella absently adjusted the strap of her purse on her shoulder and nodded, silently agreeing. "I always loved your mom. She was always so sweet and kind to me and treated me like a daughter."

"She loved you, too," he said, knowing it was the truth. Patricia Coleman had doted on Ella as if she were one of her own.

Ella glanced away and cleared her throat. "Well, that's that, then. I guess I should go."

Kyle didn't want her to leave and said the first thing that came to mind that would possibly persuade her to stay, just a bit longer. "Will you go to dinner with me?"

She tipped her head as her gaze met his again, a tiny, teasing smile curving her lips. "Will it make you reconsider my offer?" she asked hopefully.

He smiled back, enjoying that small light-hearted token she'd just offered. "No, but I can guarantee you'll eat the best pizza you've ever had and you'll go home with a full, satisfied belly."

She rolled her eyes. "You're supposed to be the enemy, Kyle."

Her tone was still playful, but he hated that she thought of him as an adversary. "I never wanted to be the enemy, Ella," he said, aching to touch her again. Instead, he shoved his hands into the front pockets of his jeans. "Come on," he cajoled softly. "It's rush hour out there. Would you rather spend an extra hour fighting traffic out of the city on a Friday night or eat dinner before the drive home? The pizza place is just a block over and within walking distance."

She hesitated, pulling on her bottom lip with her teeth, clearly torn between what she *should* do and what she *wanted* to do. He'd already felt a tangible shift between them, the anger and animosity she'd carried on her shoulders when she'd walked into his office no longer an issue. He wasn't stupid enough to believe that there wasn't still an underlying level of hurt lingering on her end, but for the most part, his apology had gone a long way in smoothing things over, and hopefully had convinced her that the he wasn't the asshole she probably thought he was.

Still, she was wavering, and he didn't want to give her the chance to turn him down. "I'd really like to talk and catch up," he said, opting for a safe, unthreatening approach. "We're going to be seeing a lot of each other while I'm renovating the building over the next few months, so it would be nice if we could at least be friends."

The last part of his statement seemed to be the deciding factor for her as she finally conceded. "Okay. I need to call my father's caretaker to make sure she can stay a few more hours with him."

"Sure." He didn't question the relief that flowed through him, followed by a surge of elation that spoke to just how happy he was to have her all to himself for a couple more hours. "I'll give you a few minutes to yourself to make your call, and I'll meet you back in the reception area."

He walked out and closed the door behind him, then started down the hall just as he heard Ella say, "Hi, Betsy. I was wondering if . . ."

He didn't stick around to eavesdrop on her

conversation. Her voice trailed off the farther away he walked, until he was in the front area of the office, where Daphne was grabbing her purse from one of the drawers in her desk. It was past time for her to leave, and as she glanced up at him, an amused look touched her pretty features.

"What are you smiling about?" she asked curiously. "Not that you don't smile, but you look like someone just gave you the best gift ever."

He laughed, not realizing until Daphne had pointed it out that, yes, he was grinning like an idiot. All because he was going to dinner with Ella.

"Maybe someone *did* give me the best gift ever," he replied humorously. Because at the moment, he couldn't imagine a better present than spending more time with the beautiful, sexy woman down the hall. He wasn't able to recall the last time he'd felt that way about a woman, anxious and excited and filled with anticipation. It was crazy that, after all these years, it was Ella of all people who inspired that sense of enthusiasm.

"Your unexpected visitor?" the receptionist guessed.

He nodded, still grinning.

Daphne looked him up and down, a mischievous glimmer in her gaze. "Exactly what kind of *present* are we talking about here?" she asked, her insinuation clear.

He chuckled. Daphne had been with the company for over a year. She had a naughty sense of humor, and this certainly wasn't the first time she'd teased one of the guys. "Get your mind out of the gutter, Daphne. She's an old friend," he said, choosing to keep the fact that she was an *ex-girlfriend* to himself. "It's been a while since we've seen one another."

"An old friend, huh?" she repeated, evidently not believing him. "Like one of your other women 'friends' who've come by the office?" She waggled her brows.

Daphne was obviously referring to the other females he casually dated, whom he'd always politely referred to as "friends," since a hookup or fuck buddy sounded way too crass, even if that's what they truly were. Dinner at a nice restaurant because it was polite to feed his date, a bit of casual conversation, and no-strings-attached fucking. There was never any pretense or promises that it would ever be anything more than that—and none of those females ever made him *want* to tie himself to one person.

For years he'd told himself he didn't have time for a relationship, that work and the company were his priority, but the truth was, he hadn't really given any one woman a real chance. Either that or he just hadn't found one who piqued his interest or stimulated him mentally—physically it was a given—for more than just a few nights of mutual pleasure.

He didn't respond to Daphne's innuendo. Instead, he glanced at the clock on the wall. It was nearly six. "Shouldn't you be gone already?"

"I'm leaving right now," she said as she brushed past where he was standing, then stopped at the glass door to glance over her shoulder at him with a devious smile on her face. "Have a nice evening with your *friend*."

He certainly planned to.

Chapter Four

GOOD GOD, WHAT *was she thinking?*

Ella disconnected the call she'd just made to her father's longtime caretaker, Betsy, closed her eyes, and pressed the cell phone to her forehead. What she really ought to be doing was bashing it against her skull to knock some sense into her addled brain for letting her attraction to her long-ago ex-boyfriend soften her determination to keep things strictly impersonal between them. But no, she'd actually agreed to go to dinner with Kyle Coleman . . . the man who'd broken her heart not once but twice now. The first time when he'd walked out of her life ten years ago and again when he'd bought the Piedmont building right out from under her.

Third time's a charm, right?

She laughed quietly to herself and shook her head. She really didn't want to be a glutton for punishment when it came to this man. Kyle had made it clear that he wasn't selling the building at any cost, so there was absolutely no reason for her to stay in the city, or with him, any longer. Even if she dreaded dealing with the horrendous traffic congestion through Chicago on her commute back home.

If she was smart, she'd tell him she changed her mind and leave. But then she remembered how he'd apologized for what happened in the past and how genuinely contrite he'd been for the accusations he'd made against her sister. And truthfully, Ella knew Gwen wasn't blameless in the entire scheme of what had transpired, which Ella had learned after the fact. But that one hot summer night had been frightful and terrifying, with her father discovering Gwen in the bathroom, delirious and covered in blood as she miscarried the baby they hadn't even known she was carrying.

I'm going to kill the son of a bitch who did this to you, Ella had heard her father, Charles, yell just as she came home after spending a few stolen hours with Kyle, the two of them making out down by the creek that ran through the woods. *Tell me who the father is,* her dad demanded.

Ella had reached the bathroom at this point, and she'd gasped when she glanced inside and saw all the blood smeared along Gwen's thighs and her sister wailing in agony on the floor with her father kneeling beside Gwen to help her through the pain that seemed to consume her.

It was Todd Coleman, Gwen finally confessed when she could speak, tears streaming down her cheeks.

Shock at her sister's confession made Ella go numb. Completely the opposite of Kyle in every way, Todd had always been a punk and a troublemaker bordering on delinquent, and he was also three years older than Kyle. At twenty-one, he had no business messing around with such a young girl—even if her sister *was* known for being a bad girl who liked whatever attention she could get from a guy.

He's the father but he didn't want the baby. He gave me money to get rid of it, but I couldn't do it.

The rage that had transformed her father's features was unlike anything Ella had ever seen before. He was usually such an even-tempered man. Charles pushed past Ella on his way out of the bathroom, his face red and his eyes blazing with contempt.

Where are you going? Ella asked before he could leave.

To make that asshole pay for what he's done, he said bitterly. *You stay with your sister. I already called an ambulance to get her to the hospital. Once they take her, I need you to close up the store for me. William has to leave. I'll meet you at the hospital after to be with Gwen.*

Everything that had happened after that had been like living a nightmare. Half an hour later, the ambulance arrived at the house, and once Ella was assured that her sister was in good care with the paramedic and her miscarriage wasn't life-threatening, she'd driven to the store as her father had requested. All the while she'd worried about her dad going head-to-head with someone as volatile as Todd, and possibly Kyle's father, who always seemed to be at home and drunk.

Just as she was getting ready to leave the market to head to the hospital to be with her sister, Kyle had arrived, and the grim look on his face and the tense set of his shoulders nearly made her heart stop in her chest.

What happened? she'd blurted out in a panic, and listened as he relayed the story.

Kyle had been home when her father had banged his fist repeatedly on the door, rousing his dad, Frank, from where he'd been passed out on the couch. Kyle had been the one to answer the door, but his father, who'd been pissed off and furious with the noise, stumbled over to confront whomever was making such a racket. According to Kyle, when Ella's father demanded to talk to Todd, his older brother had no qualms facing off with the man.

Belligerent and antagonistic, Todd repeatedly denied ever touching Gwen. Ella's father's fury pushed him over the edge and all hell broke loose. Accusations segued into pushing and shoving between the two men, and when Ella's father threw a punch that clipped Todd in the jaw, Kyle had stepped in to keep his brother from taking down Ella's father, and managed to keep the two of them separated. Kyle's father threatened to call the police to press charges for trespassing and assault, but somehow Kyle had been able to diffuse the situation.

Your brother needs to step up and be a man and take responsibility for what happened to Gwen, Ella had stated angrily to Kyle, livid that Todd could be that much of an asshole that he'd deny any involvement with her sister, even while she was recovering from a miscarriage at the hospital.

Kyle's body had stiffened, and his voice had turned harsher than she'd ever heard it before. *He swears he never touched Gwen.*

She'd been upset that he'd defended his brother, when they both knew Todd wasn't exactly a stand-up kind of guy. *Well, my sister said he was the father of her baby,* she'd refuted, her tone sharp and firm.

Come on, Ella, Kyle shot back just as heatedly. *Let's be honest here. It's not like your sister is pure and innocent. I've known guys in school that she's slept with going back at least two years. Unfortunately, your sister has a reputation for being a slut, and there is no telling who the father of her baby might be.*

Ella's reaction had been swift and immediate. She'd slapped him across the face, hard enough that her palm stung from the impact and his head snapped to the side. When Kyle eventually looked back at her, they were both breathing hard, their anger equal in intensity. Her insides felt raw, her emotions in a turmoil. She'd been so furious with him in that moment, so hurt and betrayed by his words and how he could so easily lay the blame all on her sister, that she was shaking with shock and disappointment.

The ringing of her cell phone had jolted her out of their quiet and intense standoff—the first fight they'd ever had, and it couldn't have been any more devastating. When she answered the call, it was the hospital informing her that her father had walked into the waiting area and asked for Gwen's room number, then had collapsed—from a stroke. He was in critical condition and was being taken into surgery as they spoke.

Ella could still remember how that second round of shock had seemed to paralyze her. As soon as she'd blurted out what had just happened to her father, Kyle had insisted on accompanying her to the hospital. But knowing that her dad's stroke had most likely been induced by the heated altercation at Kyle's place, the last thing Ella had wanted was Kyle, or any of the Colemans, anywhere near her or her family.

Ella, please let me take you to the hospital, Kyle had said, the biting edge to his voice now gone. *You shouldn't be by yourself right now.*

The only thing I want right now is for you to get out of my life, she'd said, knowing now that her words had been driven by fear for her father's life and anger over the entire situation. At seventeen, her entire body and mind had been filled with terror over the possibility of losing her only living parent, and at that moment in time, Kyle and his family were too much a reminder of how they'd affected her dad's and sister's well-being.

There had been other things she'd said to Kyle to push him out of her life that day— hurtful things she'd wished she could take back days after the fact. But by then it had been too late. Kyle had left town early, a good month before they'd both been scheduled to leave for college, without saying good-bye. She'd been grief-stricken by his abrupt departure, even if she'd been the one to push him away.

That quickly, that easily, it had been the end of *them*.

Ella groaned softly as it all played back in her mind. The pain of those memories had certainly dulled with time, but seeing Kyle again, and listening to his sincere apology and the heartfelt things he'd said, made her realize just how much she'd loved Kyle. That a small part of her probably still did. *I never should have left despite you wanting me gone. I should have been there for you when you needed someone the most.*

Ella believed him, because his regrets were

equal to her own. They'd just been too young to figure it out in time. His earlier words had melted away her anger and made her feel lighter than she had in a long time, despite losing out on the Piedmont building. They'd never be able to change the past, but like Kyle had said, it would certainly be nice to at least be friends. And *friends* had dinner together all the time, right?

The vibration of her phone in her hand alerted Ella of an incoming text. She glanced down to see it was from Claire.

So, how are things going in the city with Kyle? her friend asked.

Typing out everything that had just happened would take her forever, so Ella narrowed it down to the most important facts. *Well, he won't be selling me the building, and I'll explain the details later. The rush-hour traffic out of the city is horrible, and he invited me to dinner. I'll be back in a few hours.*

Dinner, hmmm? I take it you two no longer hate each other. She added a cheesy grin emoji to the end of her text.

Ella had never hated Kyle. Ever. *I think we've agreed to a truce, LOL.*

A truce is a good place to start. It could lead to all

sorts of interesting . . . things.

Ella rolled her eyes at Claire's sexy insinuation, even though her friend wasn't there to see it. *It's not like that.*

But it could be? her friend persisted.

There was no refuting her attraction to Kyle in the present, and she could easily appreciate how gorgeous he was, with a hard, solid body she'd no doubt enjoy feeling pressed against hers. Back in high school, being with him had made her feel light and giddy. But now, recalling the way his warm fingers had brushed across her cheek earlier in a simple caress, there was no denying the way her breath had hitched in her throat and her nipples had tightened into stiff peaks.

The instantaneous desire that had curled tight and low in her belly had been unexpected but certainly not unwelcome. And she definitely hadn't missed the reciprocating flash of heat in his eyes that one touch had elicited from him, too.

So, yes, Ella supposed *interesting things* could happen, except . . . *I have no idea if he has a girlfriend or not,* she texted to Claire, and could easily imagine her friend smirking over the fact that Ella had just revealed that she might have *thought about* Kyle as more than just a business adversary.

If he had a girlfriend, he wouldn't have asked you to dinner, Claire swiftly responded. *And now I'm going to give you some woman-to-woman advice. If Kyle is feeling the same vibe, there is nothing wrong with having a good time, if you know what I mean. You haven't had sex since Tucker, and let's face it, you admitted that sex with him was lackluster anyway. Kyle might just be what you need to jump-start your sex life again.*

Ella let out a soft laugh and typed back. *Are you serious right now?* Stupid question. Of course her friend was serious. Hadn't they just had this lack-of-sex conversation that afternoon before Ella had left for the city?

Absolutely. And knowing you, here's another piece of advice. Don't overthink things, Ella. If it feels right, just go with it.

He only asked me out to dinner, for crying out loud! Not back to his apartment for the night. She shook her head ruefully. *I need to go. I'll talk to you later,* she typed just as a knock sounded at the door, seconds before Kyle popped his head inside, a slight smile on his lips.

"Everything good?" he asked.

"Yes." She dropped her cell phone into her

purse so she wouldn't be distracted by any more "advice" from Claire. "Sorry, I didn't mean to take so long. I'm ready to go." She headed toward the door, which he opened wide so she could pass through.

"How's your father doing these days?" he asked as they exited the reception area and he pressed the button for the elevator. "My mom tells me that he comes into the Family Diner for breakfast occasionally with the woman who cares for him and that he seems to be doing pretty well."

Ella appreciated that Kyle wasn't skirting around the personal stuff, that he genuinely seemed to care about her dad's health. "He is, though he does have difficulty with his fine motor skills and he has to use a cane to get around," she said as they stepped into the elevator and started their descent to the ground level. "And of course that makes him ornery, but for the most part, he's good . . . except for being a little—okay, a lot—upset that you bought the building next to the market when I'd intended to buy it." And now that her plans had fallen through, she wasn't sure what her next move was going to be. She just knew there would be an alternative strategy soon, because she wasn't giving up on her goal to expand the market and bring in the artisans.

Kyle grimaced. "Yeah, I can't imagine that your father thinks too fondly of me, considering everything that happened back then."

"He suffered a lot that night, Kyle," she said, her voice soft. "He watched his daughter miscarry a baby and had a stroke himself. A lot changed after that night, for all of us."

"I know," he said quietly.

He'd already apologized for his part in it all, and honestly, Ella was ready to move beyond that tragic night and just enjoy the next few hours with him *as friends.*

She smiled up at him. "I'm sorry I brought that up again. No more rehashing that part of our past, okay?"

"That works for me," he replied with a grateful smile.

The steel doors slid open, and they walked out of the elevator to the main lobby that led to the streets of downtown Chicago. When she'd arrived, she'd entered through the quiet parking garage, but as soon as Kyle pushed open the door for her, her senses were assaulted with the loud, anxiety-inducing sounds of the city and the heavy foot traffic on the sidewalk as people hustled to their Friday evening destinations.

She tried not to panic as Kyle placed his hand at the small of her back to ease her into the overwhelming flow of bodies and to keep her close so they didn't get separated, which she appreciated. Between the crowd of people and the towering buildings looming all around her, she felt confined and boxed in. Her heart started to race in anxiety, and in an attempt to keep calm, she inhaled a deep breath—and coughed repeatedly at the polluted air that filled her lungs. *Ugh.*

"Are you okay?" Kyle asked in concern, while he seemed totally at ease with the fast-paced and incredibly noisy city life. He was completely in his element.

All she could manage was a jerky nod, and he frowned at her as they stopped at a red traffic light where they needed to cross the street, clearly not believing her.

The light turned green, and they walked with the rest of the pedestrians through the designated crosswalk. A young kid on a bike flew by them, then swerved out into traffic to avoid running into a woman in a business suit. A car laid on the horn as it drove by, fraying her nerves to the breaking point.

She flinched, and without thinking, she clutched on to Kyle's arm with both of hers, one hand clamping tight around his bicep and the other around his forearm as she clung to him, certain she looked like a frightened monkey. As if he sensed something was majorly wrong, he anchored her closer to his side and pulled her into the first alcove they came across, which was a boutique that was closed for the evening. She gulped in a breath, feeling as though she couldn't inhale enough oxygen into her lungs.

"Jesus Christ, Ella. You're *not* okay," he said, his voice gruff as he framed her face in his hands, his brows furrowed in worry. "You're shaking and on the verge of hyperventilating."

On top of everything else, she felt her cheeks heat with embarrassment that he had to see her like this. "It's the city," she wheezed out. "I hate everything about it. The noises, the people, the traffic." She was starting to pant, which only increased her light-headedness and her panic. "Everything feels like it's closing in on me."

He immediately pulled her against his chest, and she went willingly. Wrapping one arm securely around her waist to hold her tight against his body, he pushed his other hand through her hair until his fingers were curved around the back of her head, which he guided down to his chest with her face turned away from the congested street. She desperately gripped his T-shirt like a lifeline.

"Close your eyes and concentrate on slow, deep breaths," he ordered huskily. "Just relax. I've got you, Ella, and you're going to be fine."

She swallowed hard and concentrated on each inhale and exhale while he stroked his big hand up and down her back and gently massaged her skull with his fingers. Her cheek was pressed against his warm, solid chest, and she couldn't remember ever feeling so safe and protected. For so long, she'd been the responsible one taking care of everyone else and putting their needs above her own. It had been that way for so many years that it had become second nature to her and a part of her daily life taking care of the market, her father, her sister . . .

But this comforting embrace . . . it was almost luxurious. Like a rare treat where she could let down her guard for a few minutes knowing that someone else had everything under control. She'd never thought that *someone* would be Kyle Coleman, or that being in his arms again would feel so good . . . or so perfectly right.

God, she'd missed him. So damn much.

She burrowed closer, stealing a few more moments with him. With her heart rate and breathing returning to normal, the masculine scent of him filled her senses—woodsy with a hint of spice—calming her jangled nerves and elevating her awareness of him as a man who was attentive, tempting, and becoming increasingly irresistible by the second.

While her body had softened against his, she realized that he'd gone tense, despite the gentle stroking motion of his palm along her back. Her breasts were cushioned against his muscled chest in the most sensual, arousing way, and through her skirt, she felt his thighs flex against hers as he shifted ever so subtly. She bit back a soft groan when the firm bulge in his jeans pressed against her lower stomach, telling her just how affected he was by this embrace, as well.

"Better?" he asked, his gruff voice reverberating through his chest and against her cheek.

"Yes. Much better," she murmured, but made no effort to move just yet. Not until she was absolutely forced to, because this was sheer heaven. "Thank you for being so patient and understanding. I really do appreciate it." Especially since the last trip she'd made into the city with Tucker, he hadn't been all that sympathetic about her anxiety.

"Of course," he responded, as if him taking care of her was a given. "I had no idea you had urban-phobia."

"Urban-phobia?" She couldn't contain the giggle that bubbled up inside of her as she lifted her head to meet his rich, dark brown gaze. "Did you just make that word up?"

"Maybe." His eyes crinkled at the corners as he gave her a boyish grin that peeked through that trimmed beard on his face and was filled with humor. "But you've got to admit, it sounds official, doesn't it?"

She laughed, the last of those jittery nerves ebbing into a slow, simmering warmth that settled in her belly just as everything and everyone around them faded away. They stared into each other's eyes, and with his arm still wrapped tight around her waist and his fingers still tangled in her hair, the atmosphere between them changed, their mutual desire growing into a nearly tangible thing.

Slowly, she released his shirt from her fists

and splayed her hands on his chest so she could better span the impressive expanse of muscles beneath the soft cotton. He was solid and strong and well built, *and so deliciously hard*, she thought, as she dared to skim her hands a bit lower, until her thumbs boldly brushed across the upper ridges of what was undoubtedly the start of a spectacular six- or eight-pack abdomen.

A deep, tortured groan rumbled in his throat, and the fingers in her hair tightened. Holding her head immobile, he tipped her face up to his while his darkening gaze dropped to her mouth. His chest rose and fell much heavier now, as if he was trying to maintain a tight rein on his control, and right or wrong, she wanted to crumble that polite restraint.

She was suddenly dying to taste him, and the edgy, restless feeling swirling inside of her had nothing to do with being in the city and everything to do with wanting Kyle. Badly. While he watched, she slicked her tongue across her bottom lip, deliberately tempting and teasing him, and he accepted the invitation and lowered his head, brushing his mouth across hers in a soft, tentative kiss, as if he was giving her the chance to stop what was about to happen. Instead of pulling back, she parted her lips on a sigh and welcomed the bristling sensation of his beard against her skin, along with the seductive stroke of his tongue. Within seconds, sweet and gentle turned into hot, hard, and unapologetically deep.

With a low growl that sent tingles racing along her skin, he angled her head slightly and his tongue swept in and took over. His firm, sensual mouth molded to hers, commanding *and* demanding—and she could honestly say that she'd *never* been ravished like this before. The hunger and desire in his kiss were so powerful and heady they superseded anything that had been between them ten years before. This was an adult lust, filled with passion and pleasure and erotic promises. And he was a confident, sexual man who knew exactly how to make a woman ache in the best possible way and all the right places.

By the time he ended the kiss, that persistent pulse had made its way down between her legs, and there wasn't a damn thing she could do about it but squeeze her thighs together in a futile attempt to ease the relentless pang. But later tonight, when she was at home and alone in bed with her trusty battery-operated boyfriend, she knew it would be the memory of this steamy kiss of Kyle's that would eventually get her off. So, at least she had *that* to look forward to.

He loosened his hold on the strands of hair he'd fisted and brought his hand down to her cheek. His thumb skimmed along her damp, kiss-swollen bottom lip, a too smug smile curving his mouth. "I hope you don't expect me to apologize for that kiss."

She raised her brows, his touch of arrogance amusing her. "I wouldn't want you to." It was the truth. She'd been an active participant and the kiss had been nothing short of amazing, but she also knew it was most likely a one-time, heat-of-the-moment thing. She and Kyle were not meant to be.

His eyes glimmered with remnants of desire and heat. "Glad we're on the same page, Sunshine."

Sunshine. Oh, wow. For ten years, she hadn't heard the nickname he'd given her back in high school, but the intimacy of it was swift and immediate—as was the memory of what it meant to him. That she'd been the one bright spot in his life.

But before she could respond, he let her go

completely, his gaze searching her face more seriously now. "The restaurant is only a few storefronts down," he said. "Do you think you can make it there okay?"

She finally glanced back out to the main street, which was still busy, but she was calmer now, and the pizza place was closer than his office, so her choice was a no-brainer. And since she'd skipped lunch, she was getting really hungry. They'd just have to stay there until the activity on the sidewalk and streets died down. Being with Kyle for a few hours certainly wouldn't be a hardship.

"Yes, I'm good," she assured him.

He took her hand in his and gave it an encouraging squeeze. "You got this," he said with a smile that helped to bolster her determination. "And more importantly, I won't let anything happen to you while you're with me."

The best part was, she believed him.

Chapter Five

O N FRIDAY NIGHTS, Moretti's Pizza was always packed, so Kyle was glad he'd set up reservations while Ella had been making her call home earlier in his office. Since he and the guys came here often for beer and pizza after work, he knew how loud it could get, so he'd requested a booth in the back of the restaurant and away from the bar area so the noise level wasn't insane, and the hostess was happy to accommodate him. After what had just happened with Ella and her anxiety attack, he knew she'd appreciate the quieter, more private area, as well.

After a quick discussion on toppings, Kyle order their pizza, along with a beer for himself while Ella requested a glass of Moscato d'Asti—

a light, sweet Italian wine that was a house favorite. The waitress returned with their drinks, and he sat back in the booth across from Ella, watching as she took a sip of her wine. He tried not to give too much attention to those soft lips pressed against the rim of the glass or the pink tongue that peeked out to sample the Moscato. Because that only led to thoughts of that incredibly hot and intense kiss they'd just shared, which had only served to whet his appetite for more of her.

Now that she was out of the harsh and raucous city elements, she was much mellower than she had been during the tense walk over to the restaurant. Her adverse reaction had surprised the hell out of him. He'd truly had no idea how sensitive she was to the hustle and bustle of Chicago, or that it could trigger such fear and panic. Then again, other than their preferred pizza toppings not changing since high school, there was probably a whole lot he didn't know about her anymore. But he wanted to find out.

He was mostly curious why Tucker Barnes hadn't fought harder for someone like Ella and why he'd let her go so easily, even though, according to his mother, she'd been the one to end the engagement. It was like calling the kettle black, Kyle realized, and he hated to admit that his own reasons for letting her go all boiled down to immaturity and sheer fucking stupidity that had only morphed into a wealth of regrets over the years.

But now that a decade had passed, their lives had clearly veered off in different directions. He'd gone to college, and she'd lost out on the opportunity to further her education because of her father's stroke. He was rooted and established in the city, where he lived, worked, and owned a thriving business with three other good friends, while tonight had proved that she was one hundred percent a small-town girl who preferred the quaint, cozy, and familiar. She was the responsible woman who wore jeans and T-shirts and ran the family market and still lived at home so she could take care of her father.

No, his Ella wasn't city sophistication. She was sweet, ingenuous simplicity. Always had been, and it appeared she always would be. Mixing their lives now would be a complete and utter clusterfuck.

City vs. country aside, there was not a doubt in Kyle's mind that her father despised any man with the last name of Coleman, and in some ways, he couldn't blame him. It didn't matter that Kyle wasn't the brother who'd hurt and betrayed Charles's elder daughter and lied about being the father of Gwen's baby. Kyle had been involved with Ella, and he'd delivered a different but equally devastating kind of pain that any good, protective father would still hold against him.

"You look so serious," Ella said, clearing the disheartening thoughts from Kyle's head and bringing her back in focus. "Is everything okay?"

"I'm here with you," he said without bothering to censor his words. "I'd say this evening couldn't get any better than that." Okay, that was a blatant lie. Taking her back to his place and continuing where that kiss left off would elevate the night to damn near perfection. *Yeah, dream on, Coleman.*

"Still flirtatious as ever, I see." The corner of her mouth twitched with a humorous smile. "I bet you say that to all the women you date."

"Actually, you'd be the first I've ever said that to and meant it."

Yes, he'd wined and dined other women, but he'd never truly been content to just be in their company without any other expectations for how the night would end. With those dates, the final result was always sex. Casual and mutual. After he fed Ella, there would be no trip back to his condo. They'd go their separate ways, and he was already dreading the separation because of how much he was enjoying this time with her, just the two of them. He was pretty sure dinner with Ella, or being alone like this with her, for that matter, wouldn't happen again anytime soon.

She bit her bottom lip for a moment, then gave in to the curiosity touching her features. "So, has there been anyone serious over the years?"

She was trying to act casual, but it was evident that she was just as interested in his relationships as he was about hers with Tucker. "Define serious," he said, and took a drink of his beer.

Her shoulder lifted in a shrug. "Being committed to one woman for more than a few weeks?"

"Not since you." He deliberately held her wide-eyed stare, wanting to make sure she knew what she'd meant to him. That seeing her again, being with her, made him realize why no other girl had ever compared, and that was because none had given him that complete sense of acceptance he'd felt with her or the certainty that he wanted to spend the rest of his life with them—as he had with Ella.

She ducked her head and laughed a bit self-consciously as her fingers played with the stem of her wineglass. "I certainly hadn't expected *that* answer."

"Don't get me wrong. I haven't been a monk," he clarified, because he'd had his share of hookups, just not long-term relationships. "But right after leaving Woodmont, I came to the city and got a job working for a small construction company as an apprentice making minimum wage. I needed the money to help pay for the college and living expenses that my scholarship and tuition didn't cover. Honestly, between working my ass off nearly every day and on the weekends, going to school, and studying for exams, the last thing I had time for was a steady girlfriend."

"And once you graduated?" she asked, still fishing to know more.

He shrugged. "There just hasn't been any-one who's made me *want* to settle down for the long haul." He allowed a faint smile to appear.

"I think maybe I've set my expectations too high."

More questions swirled in her gaze, intimate and personal, but before she could voice any of them, their server arrived with their pizza. She placed it on a rack in the middle of the table and set a large plate in front of each of them.

"Would either of you care for another drink?" the young woman asked.

Ella shook her head, obviously keeping a clear head for the drive home. "I'm good with just this one glass."

"I'm fine, too," Kyle said.

The waitress moved on to another table, and Kyle went ahead and served them both a slice of the fragrant pizza, loaded with the simple and classic ingredients they liked—pepperoni, mushrooms, and extra mozzarella.

He took a big bite of his and wiped his napkin across his mouth. "So, turnabout in our conversation and all that, since I just gave up my romantic history, or lack thereof, is this where I now get to ask about you and Tucker?"

She blanched at the mention of the other man's name and set her half-eaten slice back on her plate. "I'd rather you *didn't* ask. I'm actually having a really nice evening, and I don't want to think about Tucker right now."

Alrighty then. So much for finding out what had happened between the two of them and why they'd never made it to the altar. "Fair enough," he said, respecting her wishes.

She finished her Moscato and resumed eating her dinner. "What I'd rather know is how you become a residential and commercial redeveloper. I thought you'd planned on majoring in agricultural business management."

Yes, that had been his original intention, back when the two of them had talked about returning to Woodmont after college. The areas around the small town would have given him the opportunity to find a decent-paying job in the agricultural market, dealing with commodity, food marketing, and environmental conservation. But when he'd realized that there wasn't anything to go back to Woodmont for, and certainly not to live there again, he'd revised his plans and gone for a degree in civil engineering.

"When I started at the construction company while going to college, I had zero experience in building anything," he said as he finished with his second piece of pizza and reached for a third. "I basically started out as the gopher and a grunt, taking on all the shit jobs nobody else wanted to do."

He gave her a wry small. "I had to start somewhere, but I worked hard, I never complained, and I learned every aspect of construction that I could during those four years while I was in school. I was also fortunate enough that the owner took a liking to me and moved me up to an apprentice pretty quickly, then full-time laborer. Two years ago, he offered me a position as a supervisor with a great salary and full benefits that would lead to being a project manager, but that was right around the time that three of my friends were talking about starting up their own business, and they wanted me to come in as the fourth partner."

"Premier Realty?" she guessed, putting her crumpled napkin on her empty plate and pushing the dish aside.

"Yes. There's a luxury real estate side to the company that Wes and Max manage as brokers, and a redevelopment side to the business, which I and my good friend, Connor—the guy you sort of met in my office today—oversee," he explained. "Wes and Max usually come across the run-down houses and buildings as soon as they go on the market. Connor and I assess them to make sure that the resale value after the renovations and improvements are completed is worth the time and effort."

She nodded in understanding. "Are you happy?" she asked, her voice soft.

Jesus, that was such a loaded question. On one hand, he was satisfied with his career. Financially, the company was thriving and he'd made a ton of money he'd invested in different ways. Mentally, he enjoyed the challenges that came with rehabbing old structures. On the other hand, there were days—actually, mostly at night when he was in bed trying to fall asleep—when he keenly felt that something fundamental was missing from his life. A certain someone to come home to and share all the successes with.

But overall, he had a fulfilling job, loyal friends, and a great life. It was hard to complain about any of that.

"Yes, I'm happy. I love what I do," he told her. "Every day is different, and there's something very satisfying and rewarding about taking a structure that is old and run-down and making it into a showpiece. How about you? Are you happy?"

"Most of the time," she replied honestly.

She gave him a smile that didn't quite reach her eyes, and she suddenly seemed . . . tired. Not tired as in she needed sleep, but mentally fatigued.

"Some days are monotonous, and sometimes I wake up in the morning feeling like I'm living the *Groundhog Day* movie, where my life feels like it's caught in a time loop. Buying the building and opening that section for artisans would have made my job a bit more fun and enjoyable because it's something that *I've* always wanted."

He hated that he'd taken that away from her. "I'm sorry."

She tipped her head to the side, her smile reaching her eyes. "You know, I really want to be mad at you for buying the building, but I can't. Not anymore. Not when your reasons for purchasing it couldn't be any more selfless."

He shifted uncomfortably at her comment. "I don't know about selfless." Finished with his dinner and beer, he sat back in the booth. "Honestly, my mom is the selfless one and always has been. Not me."

"She's very lucky to have a son like you," she said one last time, and before he could say anything else, she went on. "Speaking of which . . . how's Todd doing? Last anyone heard, he'd moved to Colorado."

"He's still there," Kyle said, then told her about Todd's DUI accident that had killed another man in a head-on collision. Todd had survived the wreck but was now serving time in prison in Denver on a manslaughter charge.

The waitress came around again, and since Kyle wasn't ready to part ways with Ella, he ordered a cannoli for the two of them to share. As they ate the dessert, they talked about her sister, too, and how Gwen came and went depending on whether she needed money or a place to stay. A few months back, she'd gotten involved with a guy who'd ridden through town on a motorcycle, and after spending the weekend with him, she'd announced that she wanted a more exciting life than Woodmont had to offer, then hopped onto the back of the stranger's bike with a backpack of belongings, and Ella hadn't heard from her since.

Kyle found it incredibly sad that both of their siblings had gone sideways, so to speak, and had only thought of themselves—while he and Ella seemed to be the responsible ones in the family. Ella had taken over running the market, not out of choice but most likely out of obligation to keep them financially stable since her dad was unable to work. She made sure her father was taken care of, and Kyle had done the same with his mother—and he wouldn't have it any other way.

As the time passed, their conversation veered toward happier recollections of growing up in Woodmont and the fun events in high school—the football games, his wrestling matches, and even Kyle and Nolan doing a stupid skit in the school's version of *The Gong Show* that got them booed off the stage. The reminiscing made them both laugh at times, and also brought on a pang of melancholy during a conversation about the two of them spending most of that last summer at the creek, where they'd floated in inner tubes and swung like Tarzan and Jane on the length of rope they'd tied to an oak tree so they could jump into the water.

Their lives had seemed so easy and carefree and fun—until the night that tore them apart in a way Kyle never would have believed possible.

He glanced at the time on his cell phone, surprised to see that it was nearly eight thirty and they'd spent over two hours talking. "I think traffic should be good by now," he said, signaling the waitress for the bill.

"Yeah, I do need to get going," she said, and he heard the soft reluctance in her voice that mirrored his own disappointment that their evening together was coming to an end.

✧ ✧ ✧

THE STROLL BACK to Kyle's office building, where Ella parked her car, wasn't nearly as crazy or hectic as the walk to the restaurant. The city was still busy since it was a Friday evening, but the crowds had thinned out, and the people now driving on the roads didn't seem to be as aggressive as the ones who'd been anxious to get home after a stressful day at work. And she certainly didn't hate the fact that Kyle held her hand securely in his, even if it was just to keep her close so they didn't get separated. There was something incredibly sexy about a man who was inherently protective, and it was so damn easy to relax and trust him to keep her safe.

Even still, Ella was relieved when they finally arrived at her vehicle, which was one of only a few left in the parking structure. As they neared her older-model and practical Honda Accord, she disengaged the alarm and unlocked the door with her key fob. She turned to face

Kyle, and he released her hand and pushed both of his into the front pockets of his jeans.

Her traitorous pulse hammered with anticipation as his gaze lowered to her lips, as if he was debating on whether or not he wanted another taste. *Was* he going to kiss her again? Did she *want* him to kiss her again? And what did it say about her that, *yes*, she'd eagerly welcome the press of his mouth against hers and the slow, deep slide of his tongue? She ached to feel his long fingers tangling in her hair and his hard body imprinting the length of hers.

The chemistry between them was silent but strong and undeniable. There was no doubt in her mind that they both felt it. Wanted to give in to it.

He lifted his gaze to her eyes again and gave her a smile that was both charming and sweet. He remained where he was standing a respectable distance away from her, his hands rooted firmly in those pockets. Despite the kiss they'd shared earlier, he was being a gentleman now, and a disappointed part of her understood. They'd be stupid to start something when there was clearly no way they could make things work between them again. There was too much history between them, too many miles separating them, and their lifestyles couldn't be any more opposite.

"I know you came to the city hoping to leave with a different answer about the property, but I'm really glad that you stayed and we had dinner together," he finally said, as if he'd come to the same conclusion about them that she had, which explained his polite behavior now.

She gave him a genuine smile. "Me, too."

"It really was great talking to you and getting caught up after all these years." He tipped his head to the side, his gaze optimistic. "I'd like to hope going forward we could be friends?"

"I'd like that," she agreed with a nod, stupidly wishing it could be more. But friends was certainly better than the adversaries they'd started out as at yesterday's auction. "I guess I'll be seeing you around, since you'll be working on the Piedmont building for a while?"

"Yes." He withdrew a hand from his pocket and absently rubbed his palm against the sexy scruff on his jaw. "I'll be there next weekend cleaning it out, and as soon as permits are approved, I'll get started on the renovations. I figure it'll take a few months to get the place done and ready to open."

CARLY PHILLIPS & ERIKA WILDE

There was no other reason to stall her time with Kyle, so she got into her car, put her key into the ignition, and rolled down her window. Before she left, there was one more thing she needed to say to him. "Thank you for taking care of me tonight and being patient with my earlier freak-out on the way to the restaurant." Without his understanding, that incident could have gone so much worse than it had.

"Anytime you're in the city, I'm your guy," he said with a playful wink.

She laughed and turned the key in the ignition to start her car. The engine turned over for a few seconds, then sputtered and died. She frowned and tried a second time, only for it to happen again. She gave it one more shot and absolutely *nothing* happened. *What the hell?*

With a sense of dread settling in her stomach, she glanced out the window to Kyle, whose brows were creased in concern. "Sounds like your fuel pump just failed."

She didn't know exactly what that meant, but it didn't sound good. "Are you serious?"

He gave her a sympathetic look. "That's my educated guess, judging by what I just heard."

She blinked at him. She had no idea what a *failed fuel pump* entailed. "And that means . . .?"

"Unfortunately, it's something that's going to have to be replaced." He glanced at the digital display on his phone. "Considering it's after nine and every auto shop in the city is closed for the night, it means you're going to have to wait until the morning to get it diagnosed and fixed."

She dropped her forehead to the steering wheel with a frustrated groan, unable to believe this was happening to her. She was stranded in the city for the night—and she had no idea how to handle the car situation. "What am I going to do?"

She was talking mostly to herself, but Kyle replied as if she'd posed the question to him.

"I have a friend who owns an auto shop fairly close by," he said, scrolling through the contacts in his phone to find said friend's number. "I'll give him a call right now and see what he can do. Most likely, we'll have to get the car towed to his place tonight and leave the keys in the drop box so he can diagnose the problem first thing in the morning."

"Okay." It wasn't as though she had a choice. She couldn't get home without her vehicle.

While Kyle made the phone call, she rolled

the window back up and got out of the car, knowing she was going to have to make a call of her own—to her father, who didn't even know she'd gone into the city to talk to Kyle. She would have liked to have kept it that way, but no such luck. She couldn't not return home tonight, or not show up at the market first thing in the morning to open up for the day, and not explain her whereabouts.

Ella made another call home, her second one that evening. She breathed a sigh of relief when Betsy answered and not her father. The last thing she wanted to deal with right now was an interrogation over the phone.

Ella asked for an update on her dad first, and Betsy assured her that he was fine and had gone to bed about a half hour ago. Since Betsy was a widow and lived alone, Ella asked her if she'd stay the night, which the other woman had done plenty of times when Ella had been dating Tucker, or the times she stayed the night with Claire for some girl time. She'd sleep in the guest room and be there when Ella's father woke up in the morning.

She disconnected her call just as Kyle got off the phone with his friend, his expression full of reassurance. "Rick gets into the shop at six in the morning. He said he'll get to your car first thing, but we have to get it towed there. So, I'll make another call and get that done for you, too, since I have roadside service and it won't cost you anything."

"Thank you," she said, incredibly grateful that she didn't have to do this on her own, because she'd probably end up with another full-blown anxiety attack. Before her time in the city came to an end, she was going to be indebted to Kyle for numerous reasons.

"Is there a hotel nearby that I can stay at for the night?" she asked him, figuring she'd see if she could get a reservation while he handled the tow service.

The corner of his mouth quirked up in a smile that was both endearing and devious. "There is no way in hell I'm letting you out of my sight while you're in the city. Not after what happened earlier."

"I'll be fine," she insisted, because she didn't want to be *totally* dependent on him. She'd like to believe she could be a self-sufficient woman when the occasion called for it. "I can handle staying the night at a hotel."

"I have a guest room. You're staying with me at my place, Ella."

His tone was firm, brooking no argument, and as soon as she opened her mouth to argue anyway, he held up a hand to cut her off.

"It's not negotiable, Sunshine."

Yeah, she melted just a little bit at the use of that sweet nickname.

"You don't have a car, and you don't know the city like I do," he reasoned, and she couldn't refute the truth of his statement. "You have no idea where the auto shop is, and I'm not going to spend tomorrow morning worrying that you're wandering around the city, lost and trying to figure out where you are."

"Okay," she relented, realizing he had a valid point, even if she did hate inconveniencing him in any way. "Fine."

He chuckled in amusement. "You don't have to sound so happy about it. Is staying with me that much of a hardship?"

No, he was too much of a temptation. "Far from it," she murmured, belatedly realizing what she'd just admitted. God, he was making her crazy.

He didn't bother holding back the playful grin that appeared. "Don't worry, I won't take advantage of you," he promised, his voice low and seductively deep. "Unless, of course, you want me to."

Her face heated much too conspicuously. Feeling uncharacteristically flustered, she glanced away from his warm, inviting stare. "Call for a tow truck so we can get the car where it needs to be and then we can get to bed." *Jesus, did she really just say that?*

A generous amount of humor danced in his gorgeous blue eyes. "Yeah, I'm all about us going to bed."

Desire, strong and tantalizing, coursed through her. The naughty innuendo caused images of the two of them tangled up in his sheets, and with each other, to flash through her mind—and she quickly tried to amend her comment.

"I meant, it's getting late and I'm getting tired and . . ." When he just smirked at her, she knew it didn't matter what she'd meant to say. "Never mind. Just make the damn call already."

He laughed unrepentantly. "Some things don't ever change. You're still a lot of fun to tease, and you're still absolutely adorable when you get all ruffled," he said, affection in his voice.

"So glad I can amuse you," she grumbled, though she was enjoying their flirtatious banter.

CARLY PHILLIPS & ERIKA WILDE

As he contacted a towing service to give them directions to where the car was located, Ella took the opportunity to shoot Claire a text.

Just wanted to let you know that my car broke down and I'm stuck in the city for the night. I didn't want you to worry when you didn't see me at work in the morning. I'll have William open up the market for me. As soon as she finished her conversation with Claire, she'd send the store's manager a quick message, too.

No surprise, it didn't take her friend long to reply. *OMG. That sucks. Do you need me to come and get you?*

No. Kyle has a friend who owns an auto shop. The guy is going to get it fixed first thing in the morning, so it doesn't make sense for me to go home tonight just to come back tomorrow to pick up the car.

Ella knew what was coming even before her friend's next question came through. That row of bubbles appeared as she waited for it . . .

Where are you staying?

At Kyle's, she typed back, then quickly clarified, *in his guest bedroom.*

Hmm. It doesn't have *to be his guest bedroom.*

Ella rolled her eyes, because she'd seen her friend's comment coming a mile away. But before she could reply, Claire shot her another note.

Considering our earlier conversation about your sex life, or lack thereof, I think you should think of this as fate. Divine intervention, if you will. She added a devil emoji to emphasize her point.

She was seriously equating her vehicle dying on her as *divine* intervention? *OMG, did you do something to my car before I left for the city today?*

What? No, of course not. LOL. I'm telling you, having your car break down in the city, while you're with Kyle, happened for a reason. Don't question it, Ella. Just go and fuck Kyle's brains out, enjoy the orgasms, and come back tomorrow relaxed with a euphoric smile on your face. You're long overdue, and I'm betting he'd be more than happy to end your dry spell.

Thank you for your sage advice, she texted back, trying to be sarcastic when, in reality, her body wasn't completely opposed to the idea of a few orgasms with a real-life man. This real-life man. Since her breakup with Tucker, there hadn't been any guy who'd sparked her interest physically. But one kiss with Kyle, and her libido had been reignited. Was she capable of a one-night stand with him? Because that's certainly all it could be for either of them.

Her phone pinged with another incoming text from Claire. *Look, there is nothing wrong with a little recreational sex. It's natural and healthy to be sexually active, and your happy vagina will thank you for it tomorrow.*

A snort of laughter escaped Ella before she could stop it, and out of the corner of her eye, she saw Kyle turn his attention to her while she ended her conversation with Claire. *We are done with this discussion. I'll keep you posted on what's going on with the car in the morning, and when I'll be back.*

Have fun and don't do anything I wouldn't do. Which leaves your options (and your legs) pretty wide open!

Shaking her head, Ella put her phone back into her purse and glanced at Kyle, who'd propped a hip against her car and was watching her much too intently—his stare speculative and his full lips even more pronounced against his trimmed beard. He was done with his phone call, as well, and as their gazes met and held, the exchange she'd just had with Claire played out in her mind—featuring vivid, erotic images of Kyle's mouth buried between her thighs as he pleasured her, and those strong, corded fore-arms braced beside her as he drove his cock into her, hard and deep, while her body clasped tight around him.

Her sex pulsed in a brazen *hell yeah*, and to

her horror, a small, needy whimper escaped her throat. Damn Claire for planting those ideas in her head!

"Everything okay?" Kyle asked, a brow raised.

She wasn't sure if he was referring to the sex noise she'd just made or the conversation she'd just had with her best friend. She wasn't going to cop to either. "Everything is good."

He crossed his arms casually over his chest. "The tow truck is ten minutes away. As soon as they have your car hooked up, we can head to my place for the night . . . and bed," he added, his slow smile downright sinful.

Her disloyal nipples tightened hopefully. She knew he was teasing her because of her earlier comment, but now she couldn't think of anything but *being* in his bed. Ella had no idea how tonight was going to play out, but she suddenly wasn't so opposed to Claire's naughty suggestion of one night of hot, anything-goes sex with Kyle.

He wasn't a stranger, but a man she knew and trusted and was still strongly attracted to. And most importantly, come the morning, there would be no unrealistic expectations of anything more.

Chapter Six

KYLE DIDN'T EXPECT it to be so difficult to try and sleep knowing that Ella was lying in the guest room right next to his. So damn close yet not nearly close enough. As he stared up at the ceiling, wide-awake, all he could think about was having her in his bed, moaning softly beneath him as he sank into her sweet, lush body to ease the ache of wanting her. And he was pretty sure he could have easily persuaded her to join him, considering the flirty innuendos she'd issued when they'd finally gotten back to his place once her car was taken care of for the night.

But while he'd bantered easily with her and engaged in her subtle—and adorable—come-ons, he'd ultimately resisted her and kept his

hands to himself, one of the single most difficult things he'd ever done. Instead of taking her
up on her no-strings offer to diffuse the sexual
tension between them with a mutually satisfying
fuck, he'd given her a comfortable shirt of his
to wear to bed and sent her off to the guest
room to sleep. The flash of disappointment
he'd seen in her eyes had nearly destroyed his
resolve to keep his hands off her.

He'd promised Ella he wouldn't take advantage of her or the situation, and he was
trying to be an honorable kind of guy. But his
unruly dick, which was currently tenting the
sheet draped over his hips, was protesting his
decision, big-time, and mocking him for being a
fool and giving up a sure thing. And every time
he closed his eyes in an attempt to sleep, his
brain taunted him with all the filthy things he'd
like to do to Ella, and with her, given the
chance.

Jesus, he was so fucked, and not in a good
way.

Knowing he wasn't going to get any rest
until he gave into his dick's demand to take the
edge off, he pushed off the sheet, and since he
slept naked, he wrapped his fingers around his
stiff length. He closed his eyes to conjure up

those dirty thoughts—his favorite being Ella on her knees sucking him off slow and deep—and just as he started to stroke, he heard the door next to his room click open, then the soft padding of footsteps on the wooden floor as Ella headed down the hallway.

His hand stilled as he listened, wanting to make sure that everything was okay with her. Five minutes passed, then ten, and when he didn't hear her return to her room, he decided to go and investigate. Luckily, his erection had subsided during the wait, and he got out of bed and pulled on a pair of black boxer briefs.

He found her in the dining room, standing in front of a window in the dark that over-looked Lake Shore Drive. The hem of the button-down T-shirt he'd given her to wear ended mid-thigh, and it looked damned good on her. He was pretty sure it would look even better in a heap on his bedroom floor, and her absolutely naked.

She seemed so lost in thought that he was extra-careful not to startle her as he came up beside her where the moon illuminated her pale skin and glossed over her silky dark hair. "Hey," he said softly. "Is everything okay?"

"Yeah," she said, smiling up at him after

taking a few extra seconds to check out his bare chest. "I went into the kitchen for a drink of water and got distracted by the view and all the lights. Everything looks so small down there," she added with a laugh.

His condo was located fourteen stories up and, in this area, was considered a prime piece of real estate and a great investment. "That's why I bought the place. The view and privacy." His unit rose above Lake Michigan and Lake Shore Drive, and there was no other building nearby that directly faced his or obstructed his spectacular view.

"So you could walk around naked with all the curtains wide open and not worry about peeping Toms?" she teased.

"Among other things," he added with a wicked grin.

Those other things seemed to pulse between them, because he knew they were both thinking about how those windows could add a whole new and illicit dimension to fucking—providing the risk and excitement of exhibitionism but without the reality of getting caught. He could easily imagine pushing her naked body up against the cool glass while he slid into her from behind. His dick twitched, liking that idea a helluva whole lot.

As if she could feel the heat and awareness rising between them, she glanced back out at the view. "You don't miss having a regular house?"

"Not really," he admitted, only because having a condo was more convenient and practical at this stage in his life. "This is close to work, I have all the amenities I need including a pool and gym, and I don't have to worry about a yard to maintain."

"Spoken like a true bachelor." She gave him a sidelong glance. "Who knew you'd become such a city boy."

He shrugged. "What can I say? I love everything about Chicago. The energy, the culture, how everything feels larger than life."

She visibly shuddered, but she was smiling at him. "And that's all the reasons I hate the city."

He chuckled, because, yes, her severe dislike of Chicago had been well established. As they stared at one another and her smile faded away, he reached out and dragged the pad of his thumb along her soft cheek and didn't hold back what he was feeling. "Is it selfish of me that I'm glad that you're stuck in the city and here with me right now?"

"No," she whispered, not bothering to hide the longing and desire shining in her eyes. "Is it selfish of me that I want you, even knowing it can only be for this one night?"

Another bold and daring invitation that was wreaking havoc with his dwindling willpower. "Ella . . . " His voice was gruff as he watched her tongue shyly skim across her full bottom lip. "You're making it so damn hard to be good."

"I don't want you to be good. I really want you to be bad. With me."

She lifted her hand and touched the cool tips of her fingers against the hollow of his throat, then slowly, gradually caressed them down the middle of his chest, along his abs, and followed the thin trail of hair that led to the waistband of his boxer briefs and the hard length of his eager cock.

He groaned, his chest heaving, and before she could cup him in her hand, he grabbed her hips and hauled her body up against his. She gasped, her eyes widening, but not in shock. No, they were fucking triumphant because she'd finally gotten what she wanted.

Then again, when it came to Ella, she'd been his greatest weakness, and he'd always given her whatever she desired. Why had he thought this would be any different?

He backed her up, and when her ass hit the edge of his dining table, he lifted her so she was sitting on the flat surface. Holding her gaze, he pushed her thighs wide apart and stepped in between, making sure she could feel every fucking inch of his aching dick pressing against that sweet spot between her legs.

He buried his hands in her hair, gently tugging on the roots to tip her head back so she couldn't look away. And Jesus, the need in her eyes, all for him, nearly slayed every last bit of his control. "Are you sure about this?" he asked, because he didn't want her to wake up in the morning with regrets.

She was already unbuttoning the shirt she was wearing, revealing the soft, delectable curves of her breasts, her smooth, flat stomach . . . "Absolutely sure," she breathed huskily. "Just this one night, Kyle. Please."

It was that last word that shattered his resolve and had him crushing his lips against hers in a hungry, endless kiss while she desperately shrugged out of his shirt until it pooled around her on the table. His tongue swept over hers, the connection turning hotter, deeper, as he angled her head so he had full access to every part of her mouth. Jesus Christ, he wanted to fucking *own* her.

With a soft, sensual moan, she tightened her thighs against the sides of his legs as she once again trailed her fingers back down his chest and pushed her hands straight into his briefs before he could stop her a second time. Her palm slid down the length of him, and when her thumb slicked over the head of his sensitive cock, already slippery with pre-cum, it was his turn to groan from the sheer bliss of having her soft, slender fingers touching him, stroking him.

He released his hold on her hair and caught both of her wrists, pulling them out of his briefs. She protested with a soft mewling sound, but he wasn't about to let her dictate how tonight was going to go, because if he gave her the smallest bit of leeway, this situation was going to be over before he even had a chance to get inside of her.

And before that happened, he wanted to savor her. He wanted to luxuriate in her pleasure and her soft, sweet moans and sighs. He wanted to make her come, so hard that her body shook with the force of it, then come again and again. He wanted her pussy to be sore tomorrow morning so she'd think of him all day and remember all the ways he'd marked her, claimed her, and had been a part of her.

They were lofty goals he was more than prepared to achieve, and he had hours to make her ache so fucking good.

"Put your hands on the table behind you," he ordered as he let go of her wrists.

She didn't hesitate to do as he requested. She braced her palms on the flat surface, which, in turn, arched her back and pushed her bare chest out like an offering. He had a clear view of her exquisite body, and he took a moment to appreciate the womanly curves she'd developed over the years. Her breasts were full and generous, her pink nipples already tight and begging to be sucked. His avid gaze leisurely made its way lower, taking in the slight indentation of her waist and the swell of the feminine hips he couldn't wait to grab on to as he fucked her.

He smiled lazily when he reached her panties, which were white silk and lace with a tiny pink bow right in the center of the waistband. Pure innocence worn by a temptress, all wrapped up like an irresistible present. He did another slow trek up her torso, and when he met her gaze, her eyes were already dilated and half-dazed with lust. As he watched, she bit her bottom lip, then closed her eyes and tilted her head back so that her wavy hair cascaded behind her and the delicate arch of her throat beckoned for him to taste.

Flattening his hands on either side of her hips, he leaned in and brushed his lips along her neck in soft, fleeting kisses, inhaling the familiar scent of sweet lemons. She shivered and sighed as he nuzzled his beard against her skin, then moaned long and loud when he placed hot, damp, open-mouthed kisses up to the shell of her ear. His tongue flicked out, he gently bit her skin, and she gasped and strained forward impatiently so she could rub her breasts against his chest.

Without pausing, he dipped his head lower and captured a pert nipple between his lips, sucking hard and strong while dragging his teeth across the hardened tip. She cried out at the unexpected sting of pain, which he instantly soothed with a slow, wet, swirling lick of his tongue before moving on to her other breast. As he worshiped her perfect tits, she squirmed impatiently and started to pant, then beg.

"Please, please, please," she chanted softly, breathlessly. And when that didn't make him speed up the process any, she finally moved her hands and clutched at his shoulders, digging her fingers into the muscle and tendons in a frenzied attempt to pull him closer. She spread her thighs wider and bent her knees back slightly so that they were pressing against his sides and she could curl her long, slender legs around his waist and pull him forward, until the thick length of his pulsing cock nudged against the damp silk fabric covering her sex.

Kyle groaned, low and deep. He was a man who knew his limitations. It didn't matter that they were both still wearing their underwear. With her using her best moves to seduce him, he didn't stand a chance, and he wasn't about to blow his load prematurely. And that's exactly where this was heading, because Jesus fuck, seeing Ella so wild and uninhibited was making him hot as hell.

He didn't have a condom on him, and besides, before he sank into her pussy, he intended to acquaint that part of her with his mouth, his fingers, his tongue. He wanted to eat her up and make her scream his name. He wanted to make her mindless with ecstasy. And for that, he needed a soft bed to spread her out on.

He slid his hands beneath her ass and lifted her into his arms. "Tighten your legs around my waist," he said, and she immediately obeyed, clinging to him like he was her lifeline.

He started down the hall, and she slid her hand around the back of his neck, pulling his lips down to mold to hers once again, the taste of her intoxicating, like a drug he couldn't get enough of. Somehow, someway, he made it into his bedroom and laid her back on the mattress. She was reluctant to let him go, but he untangled their limbs because he didn't have a choice.

"I'll be right back," he said, and went into the adjoining bathroom to retrieve a few condoms. He left the light on so that it was just bright enough in the bedroom for him to see every part of her. Her gorgeous body and especially her expression when she climaxed.

When he returned to the foot of the bed, he found Ella exactly where he'd left her, except she was about to start the party without him. She had her hand in her panties, her fingers moving slowly, rhythmically between her legs, a naughty come-hither smile on her face. She looked stunning spread out on his bed, her hair tousled around her head, her breasts bared, and her hips subtly moving as she touched herself.

He watched, fascinated and aroused as fuck and feeling as though he'd had the breath knocked out of his lungs. When had she become so damn brazen? So shameless? The first time they'd had sex after dating a few months, they'd both been virgins. She'd been more shy and reserved, and he'd been gentle and patient, their lovemaking sweet and sensual and vanilla because he never wanted to hurt her.

But this woman in front of him now smoldered with passion, and now that he was older, he could appreciate her confidence, her provocative nature. Revel in it, even. But he also realized that her indecent behavior brought out a primal, possessive side of him. One he liked too damned much.

Her fingers moved a little faster beneath that silk and lace, pushed a little deeper, and her soft, carnal moan finally snapped him out of his trance.

"What are you doing?" he demanded, tossing the condoms onto the bed to have them nearby when he was ready for one.

The smile she gave him was sultry and teasing. "Getting things started for you," she murmured.

He arched a brow as he moved up onto the

bed and between her widened knees, and still, she didn't stop fingering herself, and it was starting to make him a little crazy. "What makes you think I need the help?"

She gave a small, impudent shrug. "A little help never hurts when it comes to orgasms," she said huskily.

Her comment took him aback for a few seconds. Jesus, had she had to help where Tucker had been concerned? Did she honestly think he wasn't man enough for the job? The thought rankled, and before she realized what he meant to do, he grabbed her wrist and yanked her hand out of her panties.

She gasped in surprise, eyes wide.

"No touching what's mine tonight," he growled fiercely, meaning it.

Her soft laughter taunted him. "Yours?"

"Mine," he reiterated, and holding her gaze, he lifted her hand to his mouth to prove his point. He sucked the juices from her fingers, watching as her eyes grew dark, her cheeks flushed with arousal, and her body softened in supplication. "Your pussy, your orgasms, and your screams. They belong to me for the next eight hours. If you want something, just ask me for it, and I'll make sure you get exactly what you need."

She licked her lips, seemingly turned on by his authoritative display. "What I want right now is to feel your beard against the insides of my thighs."

The muscles in his stomach clenched at her inviting, and unexpected, request, and he gave her a sexy smile that told her that her wish was his command. Hooking his fingers into the sides of her panties, he drew them off her and dropped them onto the floor, then he settled more comfortably between her legs. Starting at her knee, he rubbed his soft facial hair up her thigh and along her sensitive skin, alternating between a tickling sensation and a more abrasive caress that he knew would leave the insides of her thighs a tender pink to remember him by for the next few days. Her breath caught with every pass of his scruff, and her thighs quivered as he gently kissed away the burn, and when he finally turned his attention to her pussy, he knew she was beyond ready to add another level of pleasure to his endeavor.

Hooking his arms around her legs to hold her in place, he fastened his open mouth fully against her sex and slid his tongue straight through her swollen, needy flesh. With a startled cry, she bucked her hips and gripped her fingers in his hair as he continued to suck and lick and massage her clit with his tongue. He briefly thought about adding a few fingers to the mix, then decided against it. The only thing he wanted filling her tonight was his cock.

"Kyle . . . please . . . I need to come," she moaned deliriously, panting, hips writhing mindlessly for release.

He could easily keep her right on the edge of her climax for hours, but to draw out her torture any more would be adding to his own. And giving her the orgasm she was pleading for put him that much closer to where he was dying to be. So deep inside her, where she was tight and hot and milking him to an explosive peak.

He pressed his mouth tighter against her, adding more pressure, more heated friction with each lash of his tongue. Again and again, pushing her higher until he gave her body what it ached for, what it needed. What he wanted— her surrender.

And it was a fucking beautiful sight to behold. Her body jolted, tightened, and shuddered hard, her thighs clenching against his shoulders as the powerful climax rippled through her. The sublime pleasure had her crying out until she lost her voice and the last of her trembling ebbed, leaving her basking in languid satisfaction while he moved off the bed to quickly strip away his briefs and slide on protection. From her prone position, her gaze fixated on his cock, watched as he gave it a nice long stroke.

"How do you want to be fucked this first time, Sunshine?" he asked, in case she had a preference.

And surprisingly, she did. Without a word, she rolled to her stomach, then pushed up on her knees so that her ass was raised high, her legs parted so that he could see her glistening pussy. The rest of her body sloped down to the mattress, her cheek resting on the comforter and her hands stretched above her head.

God, could she be any more perfect? The position was erotic and carnal yet vulnerable, telling him without words just how much she trusted him. How much she wanted him. He'd never been into the whole dominant/submissive lifestyle, but there was no denying that her acquiescence made him feel like a fucking king.

Unable to wait a second longer to feel all that soft heat wrapped around his dick, he moved back up onto the bed behind her. He slid the tip of his cock along her slick crevice, then pushed inside her, so slowly he could watch and savor each and every inch she took of him until they were completely joined. She whimpered at the depth and fullness of his shaft, and still she pressed her bottom back against his groin, as if she couldn't get enough of him.

He understood the feeling. Clutching on to the curve of her waist with his hands, he held her still and started to move, gradually withdrawing to the sensitive head of his dick just so he could drive back into her, hard and deep. With every demanding thrust into her, he could hear her soft inhalation. With every unrelenting stroke, he could feel his own arousal build tighter and higher.

"Oh, God," she moaned into the mattress as he pumped into her again. "I want . . . I need . . ."

"It's coming, baby," he assured her, his voice a hoarse rasp of sound.

He knew exactly what she needed, because he was right there with her. He quickened his pace, watching as her fingers clutched and pulled at the sheets above her head, as her body bowed and her ass lifted higher so he could slide impossibly deeper. Desire slammed through him, and he fought to hold on a bit longer because she felt so fucking good. But after a few more thrusts, he felt her muscles clench around him as she climaxed, heard her scream his name as she clawed wildly at his mattress, and denying his body what it wanted so badly was useless.

His own orgasm erupted fast and furiously, searing him with its intensity. As his release blasted through him, all he could manage was an inarticulate grunt that turned into a lower, deeper growl that seemed to rip from his chest. The pleasure that consumed him was so vivid and extreme there was nothing he could do but ride it out until he had nothing left to give.

As soon as he pulled out of Ella, she fell forward, dropping onto the pillows and burying her face into the soft cushion. Equally weak and exhausted, he joined her, flopping onto the bed beside her until he gained his bearings. When his limbs no longer felt like jelly, he got up and took care of the condom in the bathroom. When he returned, she was in the same position he'd left her in, still naked—and damn, she had such a fine, sexy, curvy ass that he was tempted to take a bite of it.

As if he hadn't just had an orgasm to end all orgasms, his dick perked up all over again at the thought, because that first round with Ella had been that phenomenal. And he was suddenly feeling gluttonous where she was concerned. He climbed back onto the bed next to her, taking in the sweep of her dark lashes against her skin. Her lips were parted slightly, her features so relaxed and content he wondered if she'd passed out on him.

There was only one way to find out, he mused as a wicked grin curved his lips. He should have teased her with soft, nuzzling neck kisses while tracing his fingers lightly down the slope of her spine. Instead, he opted for something a bit more . . . attention-grabbing. He smacked her delectable ass with his hand, the sting on his palm undoubtedly matching the tingling sensation on her flesh.

She sucked in a startled breath, her eyes popped open, and she gave him the most adorable scowl. "Hey. What the heck was that for?"

He propped his head in his hand, his devious grin still in place. "You wanted one night of sex, and you're going to waste it sleeping?"

"I wasn't sleeping," she grumbled good-naturedly as she rolled to her side so they were face-to-face and he could see the smile teasing the corners of her mouth.

He arched an incredulous brow. "Your eyes were closed and you were practically snoring."

"I was not!" She laughed and smacked him in the chest. "I was *recovering*, something I'd think you'd appreciate and would need as well."

"I don't need any recovery time." He cupped her breast in his free hand, kneading the soft flesh before lightly tugging on her nipple and making it furl into a taut bead. She made an arousing sound in the back of her throat, and he raised his gaze to hers. "All I have to do is touch you or look at your gorgeous naked body or think about all the dirty, filthy things I want to do that pretty mouth of yours, and my dick gets hard. Doesn't matter that I just fucked you."

She reached down between them and gripped his stiff shaft in her hand, confirming that he was, indeed, already fully erect and raring to go again. She looked impressed and he smirked. "Like you said earlier, some things never change," she said, clearly referring to when he'd been a horny teenager and could get it up minutes after they'd had sex.

He chuckled. "Are you complaining about my stamina?"

She shook her head, her eyes darkening with desire as she fisted him tighter, pumping his rigid length in a slow, smooth stroke from base to tip. "Not then and certainly not now that I can appreciate that staying power."

Leaning in close, she nipped playfully at his lower lip, then moaned huskily as he slid his hand between her thighs and matched her seductive strokes with a few of his own. Her pussy was so soft and warm, so wet and slippery as his fingers teased and circled her clit.

He had the perfect view of her expression as she made that slow climb toward her orgasm. The rolling back of her eyes, the parting of her lips as she gasped for breath, and the arch of her body against the hand pleasuring her. But before she could fall over the edge, he withdrew his touch, leaving her momentarily dazed and confused as to why he'd stopped.

He reached behind him for a condom and put it on in record time. Reclining on his back, he pulled Ella on top of him so that her knees were straddling his hips and his fingers gripped her waist to guide her down on top of him. As soon as his jutting erection nudged her entrance and started inching its way in, her bewilderment turned to soft, liquid lust, as did her body, allowing him to sink all the way into her pussy until he was seated to the hilt.

She gasped and flattened her hands on his stomach for support. "Kyle," she moaned softly, uncertainly.

With his hands still circling her waist, he brushed his thumbs along her hipbones reassuringly. "This time, I want to watch you fuck me and see your face as you come around my cock."

She bit her bottom lip, her cheeks flushed a lovely shade of pink. "So, you're not only an exhibitionist but you're a bit of a voyeur, too?"

"With you, yeah," he said, his voice thick with need. "Show me your best moves, Sunshine. I want to see what gets you off."

She was surprisingly tentative at first, as if she was out of practice and just needed to find her rhythm. But when she did, her confidence increased and her inhibitions vanished as she rolled her hips and undulated on top of him in the hottest, most erotic lap dance he'd ever received—and one that sorely tested his restraint. She slid up and down his cock, working him over, slowly at first, then faster, deeper, harder, losing herself in the pursuit of that ultimate pleasure.

He watched every move she made, imprinting everything about her and this moment in his mind. She was so stunningly beautiful as she rode him, and he took it all in . . . the sensual sheen on her bare skin, the wavy hair tousled around her shoulders, the tantalizing sway of her breasts as she rocked back and forth, and *fuck yeah*, the breathtaking squeeze of her coming around his dick.

Her head fell back on a soft cry, and her fingers dug into his abs as she tried to find some kind of purchase as she shuddered on top of him, around him, trigging his own powerful release. His stomach muscles clenched, and with a fierce growl, he gave himself over to the blazing rush of his climax. With a final quiver, she collapsed on top of him, limp and sated, with her arms tucked against his sides and her face buried against his neck.

Jesus. His heart hammered in his chest, and it wasn't because of the exertion or the intensity of his orgasm. No, it was something deeper and more profound that caused the rapid beat of his pulse. That tangible something that had been missing with all the other woman who'd come and gone through his life over the years. This undeniable connection. This easy intimacy. The kind of desire that wasn't just physical but packed an emotional punch, as well.

It was still there between them after all these years.

She cuddled against him, her lips feathering against his throat. "I can't move," she murmured tiredly.

He smiled against her soft, fragrant hair. "Then don't," he told her gently.

For a long time, she stayed right there in his arms, against his chest, covering him like a warm blanket while he stroked a hand down her back and massaged her scalp with his fingers, until he knew with certainty that, this time, she absolutely had fallen asleep.

And that was okay with him, because he realized he didn't want to ever let her go.

Chapter Seven

ELLA WOKE UP the next morning alone in Kyle's bed, disappointed that he wasn't there, yet grateful to have some time by herself to collect her composure before she came face-to-face with him in the light of day after her smutty, indecent behavior through the night.

Claire would be proud of her for *not overthinking things*, she thought with a little laugh as she hugged Kyle's pillow to her chest. No, analyzing the situation had been the furthest thing from her mind, not when she'd been so wildly distracted by a hard, gorgeous body designed to fulfill a woman's every fantasy, a hot, talented mouth made for decadent sin, and big, strong hands that had been both gentle and demanding, depending on what kind of pleasure he'd been trying to coax from her.

In short, the sex last night with Kyle had been freaking phenomenal. Like, off-the-charts sensational. It didn't even come close to comparing to when they'd been teenagers, and it had been everything that had been missing from her relationship with Tucker. The white-hot passion. A little sweet and a whole lot dirty. The multiple orgasms. The aching need that Kyle skillfully heightened into the sweetest, most satisfying bliss she'd ever experienced.

As far as one-night stands went—not that she'd had any experiences with one until now— it had been absolutely stellar. She'd lost count of how many times they'd fucked between short bouts of sleep, but her body, her muscles, and her pussy were sore in the most delicious, satisfying way.

She buried her face into his pillow, inhaling his woodsy, masculine scent one last time, trying to memorize it, because once she got out of Kyle's bed this morning, there wouldn't be any repeats of last night. Even if a part of her wished things could be different between them. But second chances just weren't in the cards for them. Logistically, a relationship didn't make sense, nor was it feasible. And emotionally . . .

well, there was a lot of history between them and their families that made any chance of being together difficult, if not impossible.

That was the reality of the situation, and she'd been well aware of all those variables when she'd asked, or rather begged, for just one night with him.

On that disheartening thought, she got out of bed and walked into the adjoining bathroom. There was a new toothbrush on the counter, along with a fresh towel and washcloth and her clothes from the guest room that she'd worn yesterday so everything was in one place. The sweet gesture made her smile.

After cleaning her teeth, she found a comb and worked the tangles from her hair, then twisted the strands into a knot on top of her head. She took a quick, hot shower, and once she was dried off, she put her hair into a loose braid and got dressed. There wasn't much she could do about the fact that she didn't have a speck of makeup on, but as she glanced in the mirror, she was glad that she moisturized twice daily, because it at least made the skin on her face look soft and supple.

She headed down the hall and followed the sounds to the kitchen, where she found Kyle standing in front of the stove turning bacon in one pan and scrambling eggs in another. Judging by his damp, tousled hair, he'd already showered, and he was dressed in a pair of jeans and one of those fitted T-shirts that seemed tailor-made for him and conformed to his wide shoulders and strong biceps. He put the food on two separate plates, then turned to retrieve silverware from a drawer.

He glanced in her direction, looking surprised to find her there. His expression softened as he met her gaze, and there was something in his eyes that made her feel weak in the knees. A desire and tenderness that echoed deep inside of her. Time seemed to stand still, and all at once, everything she'd tried to deny for the past hour in his bedroom now hit her like a ton of bricks—that this man's emotional effect on her was as strong as ever. She might have justified last night as a casual hookup, but no-strings-attached sex shouldn't make her heart hurt at the knowledge that that's all it ever would be. *One night only.*

With that reminder, she put her guard up and stuffed those feelings right back into the box they'd been in for the past ten years.

Slowly, he smiled, his gaze now sweet and

sentimental as it roamed over her face—a complete one-eighty from the hot alpha man she'd been with last night. It made her feel shy and a bit uncomfortable.

"Why are you staring at me like that?" she asked, not sure what had caused that look of his.

He strolled toward her, closing the few feet of distance that had been separating them. Very gently, he took her chin between his thumb and forefinger and tipped her head up toward his. "I'm staring because you look beautiful without any makeup on, like the girl you were back in high school."

For a moment, she thought he was going to kiss her. Longing unfurled inside of her, and somehow, someway, she managed to block the sentiment and pulled her chin away. "We aren't those kids anymore, Kyle." Her words were meant to give them both the reality check they seemed to need. They could never go back to what they once were.

"No, definitely not," he agreed with a sigh, then let it go. "I put a mug by the coffeemaker just in case you want a cup with breakfast."

"Yes, please." She headed toward the counter, grateful for the distraction.

"Sugar is in the cupboard right above you, and creamer is in the refrigerator."

While she made her coffee, he took their plates to the table, and she sat across from him. She ate a couple of bites of her eggs before inquiring about the reason she'd ended up at his condo in the first place.

"Did you hear back from your friend about my car?" she asked.

"Yeah, he called a little while ago," he replied, making Ella wonder how long Kyle had been up before she'd joined him. "It's definitely a failed fuel pump. He sent one of his guys to a nearby auto parts store to pick up a new one while he started dropping the gas tank so all they'll have to do is make the switch, then put things back together. He said he'll have it installed and your car ready to go in about two hours."

"That's great," she said, relieved. "Thank you."

They went back to eating, and once again she could feel Kyle watching her, and the few times she glanced his way, she caught the slight furrowing of his brow that told her he definitely had something on his mind. The quiet between them started to make her feel anxious, and her apprehension only increased when he finally spoke in a very determined tone.

"Ella . . . about last night . . . "

She knew what was coming, and she cut him off before he could finish. "Having morning-after regrets?" she teased, praying that her attempt at humor deflected the serious conversation she suspected he wanted to have.

He didn't even crack a smile. "Not a single one," he said with certainty. "In fact, I'd really like to see you again."

She swallowed hard, hating that Kyle was trying to change the rules they'd agreed on after the fact. "See me again?" She tried to play dumb, but already, her insides were in a twist and her emotions were conflicted.

He nodded and set his fork across his empty plate. "Yeah, like a real date."

He made it sound so simple, so easy, when the two of them *dating* was problematic for half a dozen reasons. Clearly, it was up to her to keep a level head about the situation. "Kyle," she said, softening her voice, as if that would take the sting out of her next words. "Let's not make what happened last night into something more than it really was."

Beneath his trimmed beard, she saw his jaw

flex and his eyes flash with a challenge. "Which was?"

Was he really forcing her to say the obvious? Apparently, he was. "Last night was sex between two adults who wanted it and agreed that it would be just one night."

"It doesn't have to be." He leaned back in his chair and crossed his arms over his chest.

"Yes, it does." She put her hands in her lap, feeling sad and strangely lost. "You and I both know that things are complicated between us. And as for dating? Well, there isn't a whole lot to do in Woodmont, and you already know I won't be coming back into the city anytime soon. It doesn't make sense for us to get involved as anything more than friends."

His expression conveyed his frustration. "Sunshine, friends don't fuck like we did last night."

The man didn't play fair. He was calling her out, and as much as she agreed that last night had been more than just getting laid, she also knew, without a doubt, that dating him would just end in heartbreak. Again. Which meant she had to issue an ultimatum.

"It's friends . . . or nothing."

✧   ✧   ✧

ELLA PULLED INTO the driveway to her father's house, parked her car next to Betsy's, and turned off the engine. It was almost two in the afternoon, but with her new fuel pump installed, her car had gotten her home without any issues, thank God. She was glad to be out of the city and back in the quiet, safe community of Woodmont, where wide-open spaces abounded and she didn't have to worry about panic attacks and feeling claustrophobic.

The small town was where she belonged, and always would. So why had it been so difficult to leave Kyle behind?

With a sigh that did nothing to ease the discord of emotions she'd been struggling with since their tough conversation at breakfast this morning, she got out of her vehicle and headed toward the back door to the house. Issuing Kyle an ultimatum hadn't been easy, but it definitely had been necessary in order for them to coexist for the next few months while he renovated the building next door to the market. He'd given her a sexy, erotic night to remember, and that's all it ever could be. A memory she'd cherish and relive when she was in bed at night—by herself.

Begrudgingly, Kyle had finally agreed to her "friends only" rule, but the intense, purposeful way he'd looked at her while he'd acceded to her request didn't fully convince her. She had a feeling it was going to be up to her to reinforce that rule while he was around on the weekends working on his mother's new venture.

Reaching the screen door, she pulled it open and stepped inside of the kitchen, preparing herself to deal with her father's confrontation. Undoubtedly, as soon as he'd gotten up this morning, Betsy had told him she'd gotten stranded in the city, and while Ella would have liked to have kept yesterday's meeting with Kyle private, there was no easy explanation for the fact that she hadn't come home last night—except for the truth.

The kitchen was clean, thanks to Betsy, as was the rest of the house, which was something Ella appreciated considering the hours she worked at the market. As soon as she placed the strap of her purse on the hook by the door, she heard her father's voice drifting to her from the other room.

"Ella, is that you?" her father asked, his tone deep and gruff, which was his normal inflection. Any softness his voice had once had seemed to have disappeared the night of his stroke. Since then, his normal, everyday attitude was brusque and grumpy.

Ella rolled her eyes to herself. Of course, her father knew it was her. Who else would it be? Certainly not Gwen, who'd been gone for a few months now without even a phone call to check on their father. No, her sister had never taken any responsibility for her only parent, and it annoyed Ella that her father was constantly hoping that Gwen would walk through that door, when it was his younger daughter who had always been there for him—taking care of him, the house, the store, and anything else he needed. It hurt that her father took her for granted, but she'd come to terms with the situation years ago.

"Yes, it's me, Dad," she said cheerfully as she walked into small dining room, where Betsy and her father were sitting at the table playing gin rummy, which they did almost every day. He'd always loved the card game, and it helped to keep her father's mind sharp and active and encouraged his coordination and dexterity.

His lips pressed together as he slowly set his cards down with a fine tremor in his hand, another aftereffect of his stroke, and gave her a once-over. "What were you doing in the city?" he asked straightaway.

"Yes, I'm fine, Dad," she said wryly, as she placed a quick kiss on his cheek. "Thanks for asking."

"I can see that you're fine," he responded, stating the obvious.

Clearly, he was more interested in why she'd been in Chicago in the first place, and without telling him ahead of time. At twenty-seven, she hated that her father still expected to know everything she did, where she was, and with whom. It was a result of living in his house, she supposed, which made him treat her as the young girl she'd been, instead of the adult woman she was now.

"If you don't mind, I think I'll head home now that you're here and so the two of you can talk," Betsy said knowingly as she scooted back her chair and stood. "There's a casserole in the refrigerator that you can heat up for dinner."

"Thank you." Ella followed Betsy through the kitchen to the back door. "I appreciate you staying the night with my father, and I apologize if he was extra grouchy today because of my absence."

"Don't you worry about me," Betsy said, her pale blue eyes filled with amusement. "You should know by now that I can handle your father just fine."

That was true. Betsy was about five years younger than Ella's dad, but she didn't take any crap from Charles. In fact, more than a few times, Ella had caught them bickering like an old married couple, and more often than not, Betsy came out on top. Having been a widow for the past twelve years, she was sassy and independent and had no issues speaking her mind. She was also still very pretty, with light streaks of gray in her soft auburn hair and rounded curves that attested to what a great cook she was.

"And just for the record, he *was* worried about you," Betsy said, taking Ella's hand and giving it a gentle pat, her gaze kind and almost motherly. "But I think your father was also concerned that you were in the city getting taken advantage of, because as soon as I told him you were stuck in Chicago because of your car, he was pretty certain you were there to talk to Kyle after what happened at the auction for the building the other day."

Ella shook her head at her father's way of thinking, that even after all these years, he thought the very worst of Kyle, when in reality he'd done nothing wrong compared to what his brother, Todd, had done to Gwen. "Do I *look* like I've been taken advantage of?" She meant to sound facetious but too late realized she'd just invited the other woman's scrutiny.

"Taken advantage of, no," Betsy said with a slight, knowing smile. "But woman-to-woman, I'm guessing things didn't go too horribly with Kyle."

Startled by Betsy's observant comment, there was nothing Ella could do to stop the mortified blush that seared across her cheeks. There was no possible way that Betsy knew how she'd spent last night, but clearly she'd assumed, and Ella had just confirmed the other woman's hunch by her physical reaction alone.

"Ahhh, that's what I thought," Betsy said without judgment. "But don't worry, my lips are sealed."

So were Ella's, because what had happened in Chicago was going to stay in Chicago.

Once Betsy was gone, Ella kicked off her heels by the back door and returned to the dining room to get this conversation over with, because it was unavoidable and inevitable. She took the seat across from her father, and it didn't take him long to say what was on his mind.

"Why did you go to see him?" he asked, his tone just shy of being surly.

"For the reasons you'd think," Ella replied, keeping her answers succinct. Her father didn't need to know anything more than what she absolutely needed to tell him. "I wanted to see if he'd sell me the building, but he declined my offer."

Charles grumbled beneath his breath, and Ella figured that was for the best because it was probably something quite rude.

"That building should have been yours," he said, poking a finger at her to emphasize his point. "I don't understand why he'd just come along after all this time and snatch it right out from under you."

Her father made it all sound so nefarious, and while Ella had thought initially that his reasons had been out of spite, Kyle had quickly diffused that notion. "He bought the building for his mother."

Charles frowned at her. "What the hell is Patricia going to do with a big old building like that?"

"He's renovating part of it into an event center and another section into a bakery, which is something she's always wanted," she said, keeping her voice neutral, because the last thing she wanted was her dad thinking she was defending Kyle's actions. "Patricia will manage both."

Her father scoffed at that idea. "Well, I don't trust Kyle, and you shouldn't, either."

Too late for that, Ella thought. She might not like that he'd bought the building when she'd desperately wanted it for her own, but she knew, and honestly believed, that he hadn't purchased the property to hurt her in any way. It was just one of those things that hadn't worked out as she'd hoped and planned. It certainly wouldn't be the first time she'd lost something she'd so desperately wanted.

"We both need to face the fact that the building is being renovated into something else," she said, because she really needed to hear the words out loud. Like a pep talk to herself.

On the drive back from the city, she'd bounced ideas around in her head, trying to think of ways she could still bring in some of the artisans without jeopardizing the grocery store's main surplus of goods. This week, she was going to do a strict inventory check and figure out what were absolute necessities and what items had been around for years and were just sitting on the shelf gathering dust and taking up marketable space. In other words, out with the old and in with the new.

She'd come up with some ideas about restructuring the store, moving shelving around, and giving the place a much-needed facelift to modernize the inside. She might not have the extra square footage that the building would have provided, but she wasn't giving up on her plans. It would just have to be on a much smaller scale, and she'd have to be more selective about whose products she decided to carry.

"So where did you stay last night?"

Her father's question demanded her attention, and like a kid caught in a cookie jar, her heart started to pound in her chest and echoed in her ears. Especially when she saw the speculative way he was looking at her. She couldn't tell if he was just curious or if he already suspected that she'd spent the night with Kyle. Or maybe that was just her guilty conscience that was making her imagine things.

"I stayed at a hotel near the auto shop that fixed my car," she said, hating that she had to lie.

But she knew her father couldn't handle the truth. It would never matter to her dad that Kyle was a good guy, because he would always see the bad.

Chapter Eight

KYLE PICKED UP his fork and dug into the breakfast that his mother set in front of him. The plate was loaded with scrambled eggs, a few of her homemade biscuits, and chicken-fried steak smothered in country gravy that she'd made from scratch that morning. Kyle wasn't shy about inhaling the savory feast, because his mother was a freaking amazing cook and he certainly didn't eat like this all the time in the city.

He'd long ago realized that his mother equated good, delicious food with making people feel loved and cared for—and that's exactly how he felt when he ate her cooking. Whether it was feeding the customers at the diner or preparing special meals for the family they'd once been, it made Patricia Coleman happy to fill their bellies with down-home country recipes and baked goods.

Now that Kyle's dad was gone and Todd was in prison, he knew that his mother looked forward to spending time in the kitchen when he came to visit—which was evidenced not only by his gigantic breakfast but by the peach cobbler she'd made yesterday afternoon so he could have a bowlful of the dessert with vanilla ice cream when he'd arrived from the city last night.

Thank God today was all about physical labor so he could work off the calories consumed during this delicious meal. Hauling trash out of the Piedmont building and gutting the place would undoubtedly burn the extra calories he'd consumed in just a twelve-hour period. He was meeting the guys at the property in an hour— Wes, Max, Connor, and half a dozen laborers who worked for the company were giving up their Saturday to lend a hand with the cleanup and heavy lifting, and he was grateful for their help since he only had his weekends free to work on the renovations, and he wanted the place cleared out as much as possible today.

He felt his belly get fuller with every bite he

took. "You really didn't have to make such a huge breakfast for me, Mom," he said, even knowing she'd enjoyed doing so. "I would have been fine with a bowl of cereal."

She scoffed at him from where she stood at the counter, though she was smiling as she piled shaved ham and cheese onto the fresh-sliced sourdough bread she'd made first thing this morning. "You're a grown man and you need to start the day with a full stomach. You've got a lot of work ahead of you, and I don't want you getting hungry in a few hours."

There was no chance of that, especially since she was also providing a hearty lunch for everyone. "And you also didn't have to make sandwiches and potato salad for all my guys. We could have gone to the diner or had something delivered."

"It's already done, honey," she said, happy as a clam as she packed the meals into a cooler, along with a container of fresh-baked chocolate chip cookies. "This way you all can eat when you want. It's all right here."

With his plate emptied—how in the world had he eaten everything?—he leaned back in his chair to let the food digest for a few minutes. "Thank you. I really do appreciate it."

"I know you do." With a gentle, motherly smile, she picked up his plate and took it to the sink to rinse it off. "It's the very least I can do considering everything you've done for me."

They'd had this conversation many times before—her genuine gratitude for taking care of her over the years. It didn't matter that Kyle insisted he'd always be there for her— something his verbally abusive, alcoholic father never had been—she was always grateful and told him so, while he knew he wouldn't be the man he was today if it hadn't been for her love and guidance.

Somehow, he'd turned out the opposite of Todd, probably because he'd always been keenly aware of how much his father's actions, and Todd's, had hurt his mother. That emotional pain was something he never wanted to put her through, so he'd always been on his best behavior. He strove to be the kind of man who would make her proud, and he'd like to think he'd accomplished that goal.

"Before I head out for the day, there's a few things I'd like to talk to you about," he said, not sure how she was going to take this next conversation that was going to shake up the normal routine she'd been used to for the past thirty years.

"Okay," she said, sitting across the table from him. "And I've been wanting to talk to you about something, too. But you go ahead first."

His curiosity was definitely piqued. It wasn't often his mother had something important she wanted to say. But they needed to discuss the Piedmont building and what it was going to entail for him to get it renovated into an event center and bakery in the time frame he'd allotted.

"So, the next couple of months are going to move fast with the remodeling, and I'm going to need your help with quite a few things to get the place done and open by the two-and-a-half-month deadline I've set for the project."

He knew it was a tight period of time, but he'd already worked out an estimate, and it was definitely doable as long as he didn't have any major problems along the way. He had a crew with a trusted foreman scheduled to implement the work Kyle needed done during the week while he handled business in Chicago, and he'd spend the weekends in Woodmont making sure everything was up to code and precisely how it needed to be.

"You won't have to worry about any of the physical stuff, but this business is yours, and I want you to make it everything you've ever wanted," he continued. "That means, while my crew and I are doing the interior and exterior construction and build-outs and putting everything in that's required for a working bakery and venue business, you're going to need to be in charge of the design and decorating of both places and hiring the people you trust to work for you."

"Oh." She blinked at him, her expression suddenly overwhelmed by it all. "Well, I'm not sure where to begin."

He smiled, because he'd already handled that aspect of things. "First, you need a name for the place."

"That I've had for years." Her green eyes sparkled with a glimmer of excitement that warmed Kyle's heart. "I'd like to call it Celebrations Bakery and Events."

"I love it." He sat up and folded his hands on the table. "I'll get all the business paperwork, permits, and licenses started for you, and we'll get a custom sign made for the place that is exactly how you'd like it to be."

A slight frown pulled between her eyes. "I

really don't know much about design and decorating. I do have a few ideas, but I'm not sure where to even begin to make it all happen."

The last thing Kyle wanted was his mother being stressed over this new venture. "I've already hired a design consultant, a woman I've known for a while who works with restaurants, hotels, and other businesses to assist with concepts, themes, furnishings. She'll help you envision what you want both places to look like."

"Okay," she said with a nod. "I really can't believe this is happening, and so fast."

"It really is," he agreed. Ten weeks would go by in a snap. "There's one more thing I need you to do." And he knew this wouldn't be an easy request for her to accept.

"What is it?" she asked.

He drew a deep breath. "Quit your job at the diner so you can focus your time on the new business."

Her eyes opened wide in surprise and her lips pursed ever so slightly, that rare stubborn side of hers making an appearance. "I don't see why I can't keep working while you're doing the renovations."

"Mom," he said, addressing her gently but

firmly, trying to be sympathetic to the fact that the diner was all she'd known since getting married, that it had been the one steady, consistent thing in her life, and it was difficult for her to walk away from it after all these years. "This is why I bought the building for you, so you don't have to work at the diner anymore. So you can do what you want to do, not what you think you *have* to do. You're going to have to quit the diner at some point, and quite frankly, I can't do this all on my own. I'm going to need you to be my eyes and ears during the week when I can't be here, and you've got decisions to make about the venue and bakery that are going to need your attention."

He watched her take a deep, fortifying breath. "You're right. I just . . . "

"I know, Mom," he said softly, because he didn't need her to explain what he already understood. "You've got this. And if there's anything that seems too overwhelming for you, we'll figure it out together."

"Okay. I'll do it." She sat up straighter in her chair, her green eyes turning more serious than he'd anticipated. "But there's something I need to ask you to do for me."

"Anything. You know that."

His mother hesitated a moment, then said, "It has to do with Ella."

Just the mention of her name made Kyle's chest hurt, because ever since they'd gone their separate ways last weekend, *as fucking friends*, he'd felt as though someone had carved out a piece of his heart that was now missing. One night with Ella, and she'd made an indelible mark on him once again, forcing him to re-member all the reasons he'd fallen in love with her all those years ago. Because she was sweet and kind and selfless. She made him laugh and feel happier than he had in a long time. He wanted to protect her, care for her, and be the guy she turned to when she needed someone to lean on. Even in their short time together, she made him want to be a better man for *her*.

And she'd insisted they be nothing more than *fucking friends*. Yeah, he was still more than a little peeved about her ultimatum, because when she'd issued her "friends or nothing" deal, there was no way in hell he would have chosen *nothing*. Having Ella in his life, even as a *fucking friend*, was better than not having her at all.

He knew the odds were stacked against them. That the smart thing to do was to be friends as she'd requested and let the idea of *them* go. But what he'd realized this past week was that he'd never let her go in the first place. Not in his mind and not in his heart. For ten years, he'd lived with the pain and regret of losing her, of wishing that things had ended differently, of comparing every woman he'd been with to her, only to find each and every one lacking.

He might have tried to bury the heartache as deep as possible so he could get on with his life, but after last weekend with her, there was no doubt in his mind that Ella was *the one* and always would be. He just had no idea what he was going to do about them when she was so adamant that any kind of future between them was impossible—for valid reasons. And right now, he was stuck in the fucking friend zone anyway, he thought grumpily.

"Kyle Coleman, wipe that scowl off your face," his mother chastised, misconstruing his emotions and whatever expression he was currently wearing as a result of his frustrating thoughts. "That girl has been through a lot in the past ten years, and there is one thing I know that she's always wanted . . . that she no longer believes is possible . . . "

"The building," he murmured, already

knowing what his mother was referring to.

"Yes," she confirmed with a nod. "I've gone into the market over the years and she's been nothing but sweet and kind to me, while her father won't even sit in my section at the diner. Not that I care, because I did nothing wrong that night . . . and neither did you."

Her tone was adamant, and a bit angry, too—not that he could blame her.

He had no idea how their discussion had veered off track to *that night*, but he attempted to steer it back in place because, for one, he didn't want to talk about the past, and two, he needed to leave in ten minutes to go and meet his guys to get started gutting the building.

"Mom, what did you need to ask me?" And more importantly, what did it have to do with Ella?

She patted her graying brown hair a bit nervously. "I want you to make a section of Celebrations that's closest to the market a storefront for Ella, so she can have a place to sell those handcrafted items that people in town are trying to make a living on. Think of it as a service to the community and helping those small businesses to grow."

His mom, always thinking about someone

else. Someone in need, in this case Ella. And the little guy, like the vendors who would benefit from Ella carrying and distributing their goods and getting their items into the hands of customers. This past week, the same thought had crossed Kyle's mind, but he wasn't sure how to make it happen. The building could be compartmentalized by storefronts, but since it was all one property, there wasn't any way to sell off a section to Ella, even if he wanted to.

"It's one piece of property," he tried to explain to his mother. "I can't sell just a portion of it to her, and she's not going to just take it." No, his Ella was too proud, obstinate, and independent for that. She'd want to earn it and know that it was *hers* without owing anything to anyone.

His mother merely smiled, seemingly unconcerned as she stood up, grabbed the cooler filled with food, and handed it to him. "You're a smart man, Kyle," she said, giving his cheek a gentle, loving pat. "I know you'll figure something out."

He hadn't agreed but his mother didn't seem to care about that. She trusted him not only to do what she'd asked but to make it work despite the obstacles. He let out a low groan, wishing that Ella, the other woman in his life, had the same faith in his abilities to fix things that were wrong and reshape the future.

✧   ✧   ✧

"DAMN, HOW IN the world are we supposed to get any work done with those gorgeous, hot, sweaty, and supremely muscular men distracting us next door?"

Ella laughed at Claire's comment because it was the truth. Ever since Kyle had arrived with his crew of men to start hauling junk out of the Piedmont building, it had been difficult not to glance out the store's front windows—okay, *stare in blatant appreciation* was a more accurate description—when one or more of them were lifting heavy items out to the dumpsters they'd rented for the day. There was a crew of about eight guys, but the only one who captured Ella's attention was Kyle. He was wearing a pair of old, faded jeans and a plain white T-shirt, but she'd come to the conclusion that nothing could detract from his perfectly sculpted body and those biceps and forearms that flexed as he effortlessly carried old furniture and boxes of stuff out of the building.

She and Kyle might have agreed to remain

friends, but that didn't mean she couldn't look and enjoy what great eye candy he was. She just wished it didn't make her feel so hot and bothered . . . and too damn wistful.

"Break time is over," Ella said, injecting humor into her tone as she forced herself to walk away from the window to get back to work. "I'm not paying you to ogle the studs next door. Besides, I don't think Nolan would approve of you drooling over those guys, either."

Claire made a dismissive *pfft* sound as she reluctantly turned her back on the exceptional view outside. "There is absolutely nothing wrong with looking over the menu somewhere else, so long as I eat at home."

Ella shook her head at her friend's amusing quip. It had only been a week since Nolan and Claire had gone out on their first date, and things between them were already hot and heavy. They weren't dating exclusively yet, but in a small town like Woodmont, where single, intelligent, and good-looking men were limited, Claire had decided that Nolan would do just fine. Which meant she was getting laid on a regular basis and quite happy about it since, according to her, Nolan wasn't a slouch in the bedroom. Lucky her.

Ella was both happy for and envious of her friend because after one extremely hot and erotic night with Kyle last weekend, her battery-operated boyfriend didn't even come close to satisfying the ache that pulsed between her legs when she thought of Kyle's talented hands and mouth on her body and all the decadent ways he'd made her come. Her bed was cold and lonely, and unfortunately, that wasn't going to change anytime soon.

With a sigh, Ella finished clearing off a row of shelves near one of the cash registers in her mission to make room where she could to carry a few select specialty items for now. She was forced to be extra discerning about what products to offer at the market, and she hated that she had to pick and choose from the great list of local artisans, when she'd thought she'd have space galore to showcase *all* the different and unique goods she knew her customers would enjoy.

"So, I was thinking," Claire said as she dusted off the shelves with a rag. "It's been a while since you and I have had some girl time, and you've been a little, okay, *a lot* down in the dumps after everything that happened with

Kyle last weekend, so what do you say we head over to the Roadhouse after work tonight? Have a few drinks and dance and just have a good time?"

The Roadhouse was on the outskirts of town and was a known pickup joint. It had been years since Ella had been there, but their only other option would be going to the movies at their one and only theater that was currently showing an outdated action-adventure flick or spending a few hours at the small bowling alley.

"What about Nolan?" Ella asked as she opened up a box containing jars of the most delicious handcrafted strawberry-rhubarb jam that she'd ever tasted, which Marylou Weber made from the fruits she grew in her own garden. "It's Saturday night, which is prime time for hooking up. Hard to imagine you giving up the opportunity to get laid."

"Meh, Nolan will survive without me for the evening." Claire thought about that for a moment, then grinned. "Or I can always make a booty call when you and I are done having our girls' night." She waggled her brows.

Great. So Claire would finish the night with a few orgasms, and she'd go home and . . . Ella shook her head of the depressing thought. She didn't even want to think about how pathetically her evening would end.

The last thing she wanted to do was go to the local bar, but staying at home and wallowing over things she couldn't change wasn't helping her mood any, either. At the very least, a drink or two would help her fall asleep easier when she finally fell into bed—by herself.

"Okay, I'll give Betsy a call and see if she can stay a few extra hours tonight with my dad." Which was never a problem. Ella honestly believed that the two of them, despite their occasional squabbles or disagreements, actually enjoyed each other's company.

For the next few hours, Ella worked on product placement at the front of the store. She added jars of raw honey from a local gentleman who raised honeybees on his farm. Her two favorite flavors were the lavender and orange blossom honeys, and she'd promised the older man that she'd carry more of a variety if they sold well.

After a while, she noticed that everything next door had grown quiet. No more jarring sounds of thumping and banging and clattering coming through the adjoining wall as they knocked down partitions and old beams and dragged debris out of the building. Claire had gone back to the office to work on payroll, and Ella cast a curious glance back out the front windows and saw that the guys had stopped working to eat lunch. Four of the men were sitting beneath a shade tree on the grass, while four other guys, including Kyle, were hanging out at the tailgate of his truck.

It was a warm day out, and as Claire had mentioned earlier, the men were hot and sweaty. They were drinking from water bottles as they ate what looked like sandwiches that someone had made and packed for them, while talking and laughing and relaxing for a short bit before they got back to work.

When Kyle had arrived early this morning, she'd been outside the store watering the pots of flowers on the sidewalk. He hadn't come over, had just given a quick wave in her direction to acknowledge her before getting to work with his crew. Unlike Ella, who'd stolen surreptitious glances at Kyle through the window as the hours passed, not once had she caught him looking over at the store for *her*. And as stupid as it was, she was ridiculously annoyed by the ease with which he seemed to be able to avoid her. Then again, what did she expect after insisting they be just friends?

She wasn't spontaneous by nature, but in that moment, she decided to do something impulsive. Heading to the coolers where the drinks were kept to chill, she grabbed two six-packs of butterscotch beer, a non-alcoholic soda handcrafted by a guy the next town over. It was one of the market's bestsellers, along with the delicious cream soda he made.

She grabbed a few of the guy's business cards and slipped them into her back pocket, then walked out of the store with her peace offering and headed toward Kyle's truck. As she neared, Kyle and the three other men glanced in her direction, and she put on a nice, hospitable, welcoming smile.

"Hey, Ella," Kyle said, his tone polite but irritatingly reserved—and she hated that he was being so *cordial*. As if he hadn't seen her naked or spent hours touching every single inch of her body or heard her shamelessly scream his name when she'd climaxed from the most exquisite pleasure she'd ever experienced.

She exhaled and reminded herself that Kyle's lack of enthusiasm was her own doing. That he was merely abiding by the friendship rules she'd established between them before leaving the city a week ago. It was difficult to fault him for that, yet she couldn't deny that it made her feel more than a little disheartened.

"Hey, guys. Thought you'd like something other than water to drink with your lunch." She lifted up the two six-packs and explained what the bottles of soda were and set the two cartons down on the tailgate next to where Kyle was sitting, then added the business cards from her pocket. "And just in case you like it, here's the vendor's information. He makes weekly deliveries into the city."

Kyle passed out the bottles of butterscotch beer to each of his friends. "Ella, these three guys are my business partners," he said, surprising her with the introduction. "Wes, Max, and Connor," he added, pointing at each man as he said their name.

She smiled at each of them while trying not to think about how hot and sexy Kyle looked wearing a leather tool belt around his waist. "It's nice to meet you all."

"Ahhh, the mysterious Ella Fisher," the good-looking guy named Wes drawled as he twisted the cap off the bottle before taking a long drink.

She lifted a curious brow, somehow suspecting that Wes was somewhat of an instigator, even though he wore a charming grin. "Mysterious?"

His eyes flashed with a wicked sense of humor. "As in, we finally meet the woman responsible for Kyle's shitty mood this past week."

Kyle glared at his friend. "Shut up, Wes."

Wes merely laughed. "It's the fucking truth."

"Totally the truth," Max added with a nod, then tipped the bottle of soda to his lips to hide his own grin.

Ella could only imagine what Kyle had said about her after the way things had ended between them, and honestly, she wasn't upset. He had the right to confide in his guy friends, just like she did with Claire—and clearly, the one named Wes obviously liked to give Kyle a hard time.

Ella glanced at the last guy Kyle had introduced, Connor, recognizing him from her impromptu visit to Premier Realty over a week ago. "I believe we kind of met at your office," she said to him, because in actuality, they hadn't said a word to one another. He'd merely given her a curt nod she'd found strange, then quickly dodged around her and left.

He cringed in embarrassment. "I'm really sorry about that day. I didn't mean to be rude . . . "

She waved away his apology. "Please, don't worry about it. It was an odd day the whole way around."

"Damn, this is good stuff," Max said, checking out the label wrapped around the amber-hued bottle. "I might have to order a case of it."

"I hope you do," she encouraged with a smile. "You'd be supporting the local merchants who are trying to make a living selling their handcrafted wares."

"Ahh, a couple of cases, then," he added with a friendly wink before finishing off what was left in his bottle.

She returned her attention to Kyle, determined to break the ice between them. "So, how's it going in there?" she asked, nodding toward the building.

"Good." He pushed his fingers through his dark hair, the ends around his neck damp with sweat. "It's going quicker than we anticipated, so we should be done with the cleanup in a few hours. I hope we weren't being too loud and bothersome."

"It's fine." She smiled at him, but his expression was unreadable. "I know it has to be done, and I know it can't be an easy task. Old Man Piedmont was the worst kind of hoarder."

"Yeah, he was," he answered without any inflection in his tone.

Could things be any more awkward between the two of them? She shifted on her feet and decided that she wasn't going to force Kyle to talk to her or try to make more small talk, because that's how it was beginning to feel, like even a basic conversation with her was much too burdensome for him.

She glanced back at his friends, who at least had been far more friendly and talkative. "Well, I'll let you guys finish up your lunch so you can get back to work."

The three guys thanked her for the soda she'd brought out, and Kyle remained silent. But as she started back toward the market, she heard one of the guys say, "Jesus, Coleman, could you be any more of a dick to her?"

Kyle muttered a reply she couldn't hear, which was probably for the best. Hell, maybe it was even for the best that they kept their distance and *pretended* to be friends. He'd been less than happy when she'd suggested the arrangement last week, and clearly time apart hadn't changed his attitude about it. She didn't like it either, but what choice did they have?

For the next few hours into the afternoon, Ella kept herself busy—and away from the front window—helping William sort through and arrange the produce bins, cycling out the old and bringing in fresh fruits and vegetables. Just as they finished and everything looked neat and tidy, two women she didn't recognize walked into the store. Since Fisher's Grocery was the main grocery in town, Ella pretty much knew everyone in Woodmont, though they did have occasional people who passed through.

Judging by the chic way they were both dressed—one in a pretty spring dress and the other in a fashionable capri-and-blouse outfit— she assumed they'd come from the city. They glanced around the store, looking a little lost and out of their element.

Ella approached them with an amicable smile. "Can I help you find something?"

The curvier woman with the long, wavy blonde hair turned around, her blue eyes sparkling cheerfully. "Actually, yes you can. My husband sent me over here to order some of the butterscotch beer that you sell."

Ella took a wild guess as to who her significant other was, based on his reaction to enjoying the soda. "Max?"

She nodded. "Yes, he's mine," she said, happily claiming him before introducing herself. "I'm Hailey Ellison-Sterling."

"And I'm Natalie Sinclair," the gorgeous, dark-brown-haired woman said with a smile. "And Wes, the smartass of the group if you haven't already met him, is my husband."

Ella laughed at the apt description of Wes. "Yes, I did meet both of them, and Connor, as well."

"I'm afraid I have to claim him, too," Natalie said in a humorous tone. "He's my brother."

"Well, it's very nice to meet both of you." Ella tipped her head kindly at Hailey. "So, how much of the butterscotch beer would Max like to order?"

"Two cases, if that's okay."

"Absolutely." Ella was thrilled that more of the soda was going to find its way into the city. "Why don't you follow me, and I'll take down your order and delivery information to pass on to the supplier."

While Natalie casually browsed the store,

Hailey accompanied her to the far-end register that wasn't currently being used. Ella retrieved an invoice pad and wrote down the order while the other woman gave her the home address where Max wanted the cases of soda shipped to. Hailey handed over a credit card for payment, and when they were done, they joined Natalie, where she was trying various samples of shea body butters that were on a small display.

"Oh, my God, this stuff is amazing," Natalie said, her eyes round with both surprise and pleasure as she rubbed a dollop of the lemon-grass-scented lotion onto the back of her hand. "I've been looking for something that doesn't leave a greasy residue, and this cream is so soft and silky on my skin. You have to try it, Hailey."

Her friend applied a small amount to her hand, as well, and they both went on about how amazing the product was.

"It's made with all-natural, organic ingredients and essential oils," she told the women. "It's terrific for hydrating your skin."

"I'm going to take one of each scent," Natalie said, picking up jars of the three fragrances on the shelf, and Hailey did the same.

Ella took them back to the register to ring

up their purchases. "So, what made you come into Woodmont today?" she asked, trying to make conversation—because the two women certainly weren't dressed to do physical labor next door.

"We wanted to give the guys some moral support and see where Kyle used to live since we've never been here before." Natalie tilted her head to the side, her gaze inquisitive. "Did you know Kyle growing up?"

"You could say that," Ella replied with a small laugh as she wrapped up the jars of body butter. "We dated in high school."

"Oh!" Hailey looked at Ella through new eyes. "You must be Ella!"

The blonde woman's reaction momentarily perplexed Ella, until she realized that, while the two women had introduced themselves just a while ago, Ella hadn't mentioned her name at all. "Yes, I am. How did you know?"

"Because our guys gripe and grumble worse than women," Natalie said with a roll of her eyes. "Wes kept complaining all week about what an awful mood Kyle was in, all because of some old girlfriend named Ella who lived in his hometown who'd put him in the friend zone when that's the last place he wants to be."

Natalie raised her eyebrows, as if looking for more information on the subject from Ella.

Horrified that she'd been the topic of gossip and these two women knew more of her private life than she would have liked, Ella buried her blushing face in her hands and groaned in dismay. "I can't believe this is happening."

"I'm sorry, Ella," Natalie said, touching her arm compassionately and pulling her hands away until they were looking at each other again. "We're not the kind of girls who judge, and trust me when I say we *get it*. Making things work with our guys wasn't easy, either. Wes and I were frenemies for years before I realized he was definitely a jerk, but he was *my* jerk," she joked.

"That's so true. Not easy at all," Hailey jumped in before Ella could say that there was no *making things work* between her and Kyle. "I staged a fake engagement with Max that he didn't have any clue he was a part of until I was caught in the lie. Luckily, he agreed to pose as my fiancé, but considering I'm a matchmaker by trade, it was all a bit embarrassing, and it took me a while to realize that Max wasn't faking his feelings for me at all."

Their stories made Ella smile, even if she

knew a happy ending like that wasn't in the cards for her and Kyle. Resolving her father's dislike of the Coleman family after all these years was nearly impossible, not to mention that Kyle was content with his life in the city, and Ella could never be happy there. She had a market to run for her father, which was their livelihood, and responsibilities in Woodmont she could never shirk like her sister so easily had.

She finished the women's transactions and gave them each their bags with their items after tossing in a few samples of some homemade caramels from another artisan. "It was really nice to meet both of you," Ella said, meaning it. At a different time, or in another place, she could easily imagine these two women as her friends.

"It was a real pleasure meeting you, too. We hope we see you again sometime soon," Natalie said meaningfully.

Ella couldn't deny the pang of sadness that tightened in her chest. Unfortunately, unless they came back to Woodmont for another visit, she knew she'd probably never see them again.

Chapter Nine

KYLE TOSSED THE last of the sledgehammers, shovels, and other demolition tools that they'd used throughout the day to clear out the property into the bed of his truck. He slammed the tailgate shut, then went to lock up the building for the night.

It was nearing six in the evening, and he'd sent all the guys home over an hour ago, once there was finally nothing left inside the structure but the framework and bare bones, which was exactly where he needed the space to be since everything was going to be rebuilt to new specifications. He was hoping the permits would be approved quickly so the new construction could start soon, and once it did, he knew from experience the remodel would go fast.

But for now, the heavy lifting had been done, and he'd been grateful for the help he'd had today. While his partners and laborers had gone back to their places in the city, Kyle decided to stay one more night so he could do a final walk through the building tomorrow morning to make notes for the renovation supplies he needed to order that week.

As he walked toward the large double doors leading into the new event center, he cast a surreptitious glance over at the market, which was also shutting down for the night. Employees were pulling in items from the sidewalk, and Kyle could see William, the longtime manager, cashing out the registers while the younger clerks wiped down counters and straightened products on the shelves.

Kyle pulled out the keys to the building and secured the doors and lock, debating on whether or not to head over to the store to talk to Ella and apologize to her, because as much as he hated to admit it, Wes had been right in calling him a dick for his behavior toward her during their lunch break. The woman made him crazy, and his purpose for being so abrupt with Ella was to show her that he was just fine and dandy with that *fucking friends* request she'd issued.

But he so wasn't okay with any of it. Having her so close was like being taunted with the sweetest piece of candy but being told he could only look at the delicious, tempting, sugary treat because it wasn't his to touch or taste. And fuck, he wanted to touch and taste Ella again in the worst way possible, and knowing that he'd been banned from indulging his sweet tooth had made him a stupid, pouty, and irritable brat, like a recalcitrant little boy who hadn't gotten his way.

Yeah, definitely not one of his finer moments.

He wasn't sure if she was still at the store or if she'd already headed home and her employees were shutting everything down for the night. Hell, he didn't even know if she'd talk to him after the ass he'd been.

Not sure what he wanted to do, he exhaled a deep sigh as his cell pinged with a text notification. He pulled the phone from his pocket and read the message from Nolan.

Hey. You mentioned that you're staying in town until tomorrow morning when I saw you earlier. Got any plans for tonight? his friend asked.

Other than heading back to his mom's, eating dinner, and taking a long, hot shower to wash away the sweat and grime, his night was pretty wide-open. *No, not really. What's up?* he typed back.

I thought we could head over to the Roadhouse and have a few beers.

Kyle groaned. The only reason a guy went to the Roadhouse was to try his best to get laid, and knowing what it was like to be deep inside of Ella, the thought of being with another woman any time soon left a bad taste in his mouth. It would be like trading in fine champagne for cheap tequila, and he'd discovered that he fucking *loved* the taste of champagne.

I'm not sure I'm in the mood . . .

Oh, did I forget to mention that Claire happened to tell me that she was going to be there with Ella tonight? Something about a girls' night out . . .

Kyle felt the hairs on the back of his neck bristle. Well, that certainly had him reassessing his answer, because the only thought in his mind was imagining some asshole coming on to Ella, and he'd fucking kill anyone who touched her.

If Claire is going with Ella, then why are you going? he asked curiously.

Why the fuck do you think? I want to keep an eye on Claire, but if I go alone I'm going to look like a goddamn stalker, so I need it to look like I'm there for a casual night out with a bro. We'll keep a low profile and let the girls have their fun, but I, personally, want to make sure no one messes with what's mine.

Damn, Kyle definitely understood that territorial feeling, like something was clawing his insides to shreds. *Are you and Claire exclusive?*

No, but that's not the point, Nolan replied, clearly not giving a shit that he and Claire had yet to have that committed-relationship conversation.

Wouldn't it be easier if you did make things exclusive with her, instead of tailing her wherever she goes like a creeper? Kyle smirked as he hit the send button. Okay, now he was just giving his friend shit, because Nolan was obviously into Claire in a big way, and the situation was clearly making the other man a little crazed.

Look, I only just realized I want to be exclusive with Claire. Like the moment she texted me to tell me that she wouldn't be able to see me tonight because she was going out with Ella to the fucking Roadhouse. The fact that I'm feeling possessive as hell pretty much says I'm fucked where she's concerned.

Kyle chuckled as he replied. *Roger that.*

Good. So, are you in or not?

I'm in. Kyle hoped to God he didn't regret his decision. He wasn't sure he could even handle watching another man talking to Ella, knowing that the guy was probably mentally undressing her as they spoke.

I'll pick you up at nine, Kyle added. Which was when the place really started getting busy on a Saturday night.

By the time he was done texting with Nolan, most of the lights at the market had been shut off, so he nixed the idea he'd had to go and apologize to Ella. If he was going to see her at the Roadhouse anyway, he figured that would be just as good of a time, and a great excuse, to talk to her and keep her occupied so no other guy had a chance.

✧   ✧   ✧

FINDING A PARKING spot at the Roadhouse on a Saturday night was nearly impossible. The designated area was packed with vehicles, forcing Kyle to park his truck in the next grassy lot over and him and Nolan to make the extra trek to the bar.

After leaving the new Celebrations building, Kyle had driven to his mother's and gone through the routine he'd already had in mind—he'd eaten the pot roast dinner his mom had waiting for him and spent an hour talking with her about the day while they'd enjoyed the meal together. Then, he'd taken that long, hot shower, and since he'd had the time, he'd shaved his neck and trimmed his beard and added a splash of cologne. He'd dressed casually, in dark jeans and a black T-shirt, because tonight was supposed to be about having a beer or two with a friend, and nothing more. Oh, while keeping an eye on Ella. Yeah, that, too.

Kyle glanced over at Nolan, who wasn't wasting any time getting to the building that was already reverberating from the loud music playing inside. "You do realize, don't you, that this plan of yours could backfire?" he asked, wanting to make sure his friend was aware of the liability inherent in his plan. "That Claire could get pissed as hell that you're crashing her girls' night out?" As for Ella—Kyle reasoned that she'd already relegated him to platonic status, so he shouldn't pose a threat to her having a fun evening, right?

"It's a risk I'm willing to take," Nolan replied, nonplussed, before following that up with a confident smirk. "Besides, I already know that the makeup sex will be worth it."

Kyle just shook his head, but damned if he wasn't a bit envious of his friend's certainty and attitude. At least one of them was going to get lucky with the woman they wanted tonight.

Nolan opened the door, and they were instantly blasted by the obnoxiously loud rock song blaring from the speakers mounted around the open, spacious establishment. They made their way inside, and Kyle realized that he was too old for this shit. That going to an overly crowded bar for a beer was highly overrated when he could have a drink in the peace and quiet of his own home. But he reminded himself he had a purpose tonight, and now that he was here, he found himself already glancing around for Ella's familiar face.

He was at least a foot taller than most adults, but it was still difficult to see anything more than the tops of people's heads and discern whether they were male or female, which only served to frustrate Kyle. The ground level, where he and Nolan were currently, was overpopulated due to the bar setup, standing tabletops, and dance area that everyone wanted to be near. Remembering there was a second-tier balcony that overlooked the entire first floor, he looked up, grateful to find that it was far less busy and the perfect place to keep an eye on anything and everything—and anyone. Once he found her.

Catching Nolan's attention, Kyle made an *I'm going upstairs* gesture with the hitch of his thumb, and his friend nodded. Up above, they found a vacant table at the far end of the balcony that was next to the railing, and claimed it for themselves. As soon as they were seated, a cocktail waitress took their orders for two beers on tap, then went to retrieve their drinks.

Kyle didn't waste time before combing through the crowd below, and Nolan did the same. It took him a few minutes, but he finally found Ella and Claire tucked away in their own corner downstairs, diagonally to where he and Nolan were positioned. He nudged his friend and pointed out the girls' location, and now that they had them in view, they both sat back in their chairs and relaxed. Their beer arrived, which Kyle paid for while also giving the server a generous tip.

They were good to go, their surveillance underway, and the girls none the wiser.

It was too loud for a normal conversation with Nolan, so for the next forty minutes, the two of them drank their beer and kept their attention on Claire and Ella. For the most part, the women kept to themselves, and no one bothered them, either. They leaned in close as they chatted and leisurely sipped what looked like one of those frilly, fruity martini-type cocktails.

After a while, when they both stood up, Kyle tracked their progress to the crowded dance floor and exhaled a relieved breath when they started to dance . . . with each other. There were other girls doing the same, and he found himself smiling as he watched Ella from afar, seemingly happy and carefree for the moment as she and Claire shimmied against each other, laughing and enjoying their evening.

Half a dozen songs later, they made their way through the growing throng of people filling the dance floor. Ella said something to Claire, who nodded and went in the direction of the table they'd been sitting at, while Ella went up to the bar and ordered a drink from the bartender. He set a bottle of water on the counter, and she twisted the cap off and took a long, thirsty drink just as a guy came up beside her.

Kyle stiffened in his seat when Ella's face lit

up and she gave the other man a warm, too-intimate hug. He narrowed his gaze as they broke apart, allowing him the chance to take a closer look at the guy's features . . . and to realize it was her ex-fiancé, Tucker Barnes. She might have ended her engagement to him, but there didn't appear to be any animosity between them. In fact, Kyle didn't care for the way she was smiling at the other man or the easy, familiar way Tucker touched her bare arm.

Kyle stood so abruptly that his chair scraped back on the wooden floor, his entire body so tense he felt his shirt tighten against his chest and arms. Nolan immediately jumped up beside him and pressed his fingers against Kyle's chest to hold him back.

"Whoa! Jesus, you look like the fucking Hulk, and you need to calm down," Nolan said, clearly trying to be the voice of reason. "Don't go charging down there like a bull in a china shop."

Kyle raised an irritable brow at his friend. "Tell me you wouldn't feel the same way if it was Claire greeting an ex so enthusiastically."

"Okay, point taken," Nolan said, backing off slightly. "Tucker isn't a bad guy, so don't do something stupid you'll regret later, like planting your fist against his jaw."

Kyle wasn't going to hurt the guy, but he was going to stake a goddamn claim on what was his and make sure that Tucker knew it. "You go and take care of Claire while I go and . . . diffuse the situation with Tucker. Swear to God, I won't touch him."

"Fine," Nolan said, and they both headed toward the stairs.

When they reached the first floor, Nolan veered to the right, where Claire had gone, and Kyle strode directly to the far end of the bar, where Tucker and Ella were talking. Tucker was smiling at her in a way that made Kyle's blood run hot in his veins and told him that the other man might not be over the woman he'd been engaged to marry. From what he recalled, Ella had been the one to end things, not Tucker.

As he'd promised Nolan, Kyle cooled his jets as he came up beside Ella, surprising the two of them with his sudden appearance, which he took full advantage of. Ella was staring at him with big, where-the-hell-did-you-come-from eyes, but before she could say anything, Kyle stuck his hand out for the other man to shake.

See, he could totally be courteous and amicable.

"Hey, Tucker," Kyle said in an easygoing voice that belied the instinct to beat on his chest like a caveman before flipping Ella over his shoulder and whisking her away. "Good to see you."

"Uhh, you, too, Kyle." Tucker winced slightly at the crushing strength of Kyle's fingers wrapped around his hand and visibly relaxed when they finally let go. "It's been a long time. I heard you bought the old Piedmont building."

"Sure did." The last thing Kyle wanted to do was make small talk with the other man, even if they had grown up together and attended the same high school. "If you don't mind, I'm going to steal Ella away for a dance."

Ella sputtered a reply—or a protest, it was difficult to tell which—and even when Kyle grasped her elbow to lead her into the fray, he could feel her resistance. There were so many people dancing that they were pushed close together, and he took advantage of the situation to secure an arm around her waist and align their bodies from stomach to thighs.

Ella's eyes flashed with indignation, and fuck if her red-hot attitude didn't make him hard. Her face was flushed, a light sheen of perspiration dotted her skin, and her gorgeous breasts heaved above the low-cut, formfitting top she was wearing that showed off way too much cleavage to the male population.

"What the hell was that?" Ella shouted to be heard while pushing against his shoulders with the flat of her hand to separate them, to no avail. "And what are you doing here?"

Because of the loud music, he dipped his head close to her ear as he slid his free hand into the thick, silky hair she'd left unbound for the night, wrapping it around his fist just because he could. "Apparently, I'm saving you from your ex."

She jerked her head back, but not very far considering his fingers had a firm grip on her hair. But enough that she could look up at him and he could see the fire in her gaze. "Don't be a *dick*," she said, taunting him with the insult that Wes had used to call him out on his behavior toward her today. "Regardless of what happened between Tucker and me, he's still a friend. Not that it's any of your business!"

That fucking word grated on his nerves like nails screeching down a chalkboard. "You sure do collect a lot of *friends*," he drawled in an insolent tone, even as he realized that this conversation was no longer about Tucker and all about the two of them. "And the problem is, as you already know, I don't want to be your *fucking friend*." He emphasized the point by sliding his hand possessively over the curve of her butt in those tight black jeans she was wearing so he could grind the hard length of his cock against her mound.

She squirmed in his hold and bucked her hips against his to try and break free, but between his strength and the help of the people around them inadvertently pushing him and Ella together, she wasn't going anywhere until he decided she was.

Her chin tipped up obstinately, and she gave him a devious smile that was a little too smug for his liking. "Is that why you had a stick up your ass this afternoon when I came next door to say hi?"

His jaw clenched, the push-pull of sexual tension between them suddenly incendiary. He only needed to strike a match to make it blaze out of control, and he didn't hesitate to do just that. "Goddamn sassy mouth," he growled, forcing her head back another few inches until her parted lips were right below his. "I can think of a half a dozen better uses for it than hurling insults at me."

She huffed out a sarcastic laugh to deliberately mock him. "Dream on, *City Boy*."

Her remark was both a dare and a challenge. It was also the final spark that had his own smoldering frustration boiling over and combusting between them in spectacular fashion. The next second, he had his fingers secured around one of her wrists. He pulled her behind him through the dance crowd, giving her no choice but to follow him to the exit at the backside of the building, then out into the cool night air that did nothing to take the edge off the heat and lust pumping through his veins.

Ignoring the few people outside who were either smoking a cigarette or taking a break from the raucous atmosphere in the bar, Kyle continued through the main parking area and onto the adjoining grassy lot where he'd had to park. Ella didn't protest or resist, and it was a damn good thing because he wasn't opposed to following through on his earlier thought to heft her over his shoulder like fucking Tarzan.

He drew her around to the passenger side of the truck, which faced away from the bar and any prying eyes, and backed her up against the door. He caught her face in his hands and forced her gaze to meet his. They were both breathing hard, and while he saw a trace of defiance in her bright green eyes, there was something else there, too—a desire and need that told him she was equally turned on.

"You want to know what this *city boy* dreams about, baby?" he taunted in a raspy voice hoarse with carnality. "You. All fucking week long, every goddamn night, I dream about *you*."

Her tongue licked across her bottom lip, dampening it and drawing his attention to her lush, sexy mouth. "Doing what?"

She was tempting and teasing him, but what she didn't realize was that he was far better at this game than she was. "You, flat on your back with your legs spread wide while I'm driving into your soft, warm body. You, writhing beneath me, wanting more, harder, deeper, and I give you every single inch I've got."

A soft moan escaped her throat as her hands went to the waistband of his jeans, her fingers fumbling with the button until it came undone. "What else?" she asked huskily.

She'd unzipped his pants and pushed his jeans and briefs down his hips until his thick erection sprang free. He groaned when she wrapped her cool fingers around his rock-hard flesh and stroked him in her palm.

"*What else*, City Boy?" she prompted again,

more demanding this time.

She skimmed her thumb over the head of his shaft, already slick with a bead of fluid. His entire body jerked from the pleasure of it, and his mind struggled to stay focused on seducing *her*. "I dream about you on your knees while I do dirty, sinful things to your mouth with my cock. I fucking *ache* to feel your lips sliding up and down my dick as you suck me off."

Before he realized her intent, she dropped to her knees in front of him on the grass and had his cock right where he wanted it to be— needed it to be—deep in her mouth, her lips rimming the width as she glided down and her tongue lapping along the length as she pulled back up, nice and torturously slow.

"Jesus," he choked out, realizing that his Ella had just turned the tables on him, the seducer becoming the seduced as she continued sucking him, licking him—squeezing his goddamn balls in her hand—and making his erotic dream a reality right here and now.

With a deep, guttural groan, he braced his palms on the doorframe and glanced down, grateful for the small amount of moonlight that enabled him to witness this moment. With a small tip of her head, she was looking up at him, too, her eyes dark and sultry, and he could have sworn there was a wicked smile curving her lips as she dragged them back up the length of his cock once again.

Hot, pulsing anticipation rolled through him, and he instinctively flexed his hips, working his way back into the incredible heat enveloping him. He continued to watch her perfect mouth take him deep, sucking him and fucking swallowing him when the head hit the back of her throat.

He hissed out a breath, the muscles in his stomach tightening in warning. "Ella . . . Jesus, *fuck*, I'm going to come," he struggled to say, wanting to give her time to stop before he blew his load so she could finish him off with her hand instead.

She made a soft, sensual sound and merely took him deeper, stroked him harder, sucked him stronger, and there was nothing he could do to halt the surge of his orgasm as it pummeled through him. Squeezing his eyes shut, he clenched his jaw and grunted as he came, his body shuddering as the indescribable pleasure seemed to short-circuit his brain.

When he was no longer seeing stars, he opened his eyes to find that Ella was no longer on her knees in front of him... she was walking *away* from him, already a few car lengths in distance. *What the fuck?* His satisfied dick was still hanging out of his jeans, and he shook his head to clear it while he tucked himself back in.

"Ella!" he called out, but she ignored him as he tried to pull up his zipper, only to realize it was stuck and had snagged on his briefs. *Fucking great.* He certainly wasn't going to chase after her with his pants flapping open, and he cursed as he tugged on the cotton material but couldn't extract it from the metal teeth of his zipper.

"Ella?"

Kyle recognized Claire's concerned voice, and he glanced across the bed of his truck to see the other woman walking in Ella's direction from the main parking lot, with Nolan accompanying her.

"Is everything okay?" Claire asked as she reached Ella. The other woman's gaze lifted to where Kyle was standing on the other side of his truck, then returned to her friend. "I was worried when I couldn't find you inside."

"Everything is fine," Ella assured her, though she didn't sound *fine*. "I need you to take me home."

"Sure thing," her friend said as the two of them headed toward Claire's car.

"Ella, dammit, *wait!*" Kyle tried again, hating the desperation in his voice.

Of course, she didn't so much as slow her steps or give any indication that she heard him. Frustration shortened his temper, and he yanked hard enough to rip fabric out of the zipper, but by then it was too late. The two of them were in Claire's car and she was already backing out of the spot.

And to further his humiliation, Nolan was now standing in front of him, chuckling as he realized why the fly of Kyle's pants was still wide-open.

"At least it wasn't your dick that got caught in your zipper," Nolan said humorously.

Kyle wasn't in the mood. "Shut the fuck up and get in the truck. I'm taking you home."

And then he was going to go and find out what the hell had just happened with Ella.

Chapter Ten

ELLA QUIETLY UNLOCKED the front door to the house she'd grown up in and stepped inside the living room, where Betsy was reading a book on the couch. Since the older woman was alone and it was after ten, Ella assumed that her father had already turned in for the night.

Betsy closed her book and Ella smiled at the other woman. "Thanks for staying with my dad again. It was nice to get out for a while." And it had been nice and fun and relaxing, until Kyle had shown up and not only tried to start a pissing contest with Tucker, but then he'd provoked her into breaking her own damn rules about them being friends.

God, she was so weak when it came to him.

"Anytime, dear. You know that." Betsy stood and gathered her purse and the knitting bag she always brought with her. "But your father is more than capable of taking care of himself and really doesn't need me here all the time. You do realize that, right?"

Ella blinked at her, surprised by the comment. "He has a hard time getting around, and I want to make sure that he has help nearby when I'm not here." She'd never forgive herself if her father slipped and fell or had some kind of accident because of his lack of motor skills and ended up hurting himself.

Betsy shook her head, though she was smiling. "He gets around just fine. Quite honestly, for a long time now I've suspected that he acts frail and incapable because you've always catered to him. He won't wither away if you go out and live your life, and that's what you *should* be doing. You're a young woman. You need to find yourself a man, get married, and have your own family."

Ella wasn't sure what had brought on this conversation, but it caused an odd tightness in her chest. She'd *tried* to find a man, had nearly gotten married, only to realize how unfair it would all be to Tucker, to tie him to her burdens and her schedule. Not that she considered her father a burden, but still. And to be honest, she'd never felt about him the way she felt about . . . No. She wasn't going there. But she hadn't loved Tucker the way they both deserved if she were going to marry him.

As for her father . . . she knew there was truth to what Betsy was saying, but her own guilty conscience and that sense of responsibility she'd carried since her mother's death and then her father's stroke was hard to let go. She couldn't let something happen to him if she could avoid it by having Betsy around. And her father depended on her to keep the store running, to keep the mortgage paid, and unfortunately, there was no one else around to share the burden that had, over the years, become hers and hers alone.

She walked Betsy out to her car, and once the other woman was gone, Ella headed back into the house and locked the door. She took a hot shower, changed into one of the soft, comfy tank-top-and-short sets she slept in, then climbed into bed after turning off all the lights. The house was quiet, and since she was wide-awake, her mind insisted on replaying everything that had happened with Kyle tonight.

CARLY PHILLIPS & ERIKA WILDE

She'd never intended for anything to happen between them, but the chemistry and attraction between them was impossible to resist. And God, that show of dominance of his that she'd glimpsed had excited and thrilled her, and because she'd still been annoyed with him after his cool attitude toward her that afternoon, it had been so easy to engage him, to let all that sexual tension turn all that frustration into something hot and steamy and physical.

Except it hadn't stayed all about the physical pleasure and release. Not for her. No, her stupid emotions had wheedled their way into where they didn't belong.

She'd walked away after his orgasm not to prove the point that she *could*, but because she'd felt *too much* in that moment. She'd been overwhelmed by the intensity of their encounter and addicted to how amazing it felt to give him that ultimate pleasure. She'd walked away because she was terrified that she was falling in love with Kyle again, and that was a dangerous thing for her heart to do.

A soft *tap, tap, tap* at her window startled her out of her thoughts and also made her traitorous heart flutter, because she *knew* what that *tap, tap, tap* meant. And *who* was making the noise, despite the fact that the curtains were drawn and she couldn't see outside. It took her back to when she and Kyle were dating in high school, and he'd sneak into her bedroom at night exactly like this, and with the house being a one-story, getting in and out had been ridiculously easy for him to do.

Tap, tap, tap. She wanted to ignore him, but the sound was a little louder this time, definitely more impatient, and after the way she'd walked away from him without a word or explanation back at the Roadhouse, she knew he wasn't going to give up anytime soon.

Tossing off the covers, she padded over to the window and pushed aside the curtain. Sure enough, Kyle was standing on the other side of the glass, and he'd already removed the screen from the frame. *Yeah, just like old times.*

"I already gave you a blow job. What else do you want?" she asked in an annoyed whisper.

He glared at her, his hands on his hips. "Open the goddamn window," he hissed, and it was the fear that he'd wake up her father—even though his bedroom was on the opposite side of the house—that had her obeying his command. She wasn't about to take any chances.

As quietly as possible, she unlatched the

wooden frame, and while Kyle pushed it up and climbed through the opening, she went to her bedroom door and jammed a rubber wedge beneath it to make sure no one could open it from the hallway, just as a precaution. The house had been built in the early 1920s, and the doors didn't have locks. Growing up, her parents had preferred it that way. And as an adult, she'd never had a reason to install one. Until now.

She turned around to face Kyle, who looked much too imposing in her bedroom. She'd kept the lights off, but she could see him easily enough, and his tense body language spoke for itself.

"Care to explain what happened back at the Roadhouse?" he asked in a low voice that vibrated with annoyance.

She crossed her arms over her chest and shifted on her bare feet. "No, not really." How did she put into words how confused and conflicted she felt? She couldn't explain it to herself, let alone him.

"*Try*," he insisted, his gaze narrowed as he took a step closer.

She took a step back. "I can't." Her throat felt as raw as her emotions.

Something in his expression changed, softened, and this time when he moved closer, she didn't retreat. He reached up and tucked a strand of hair behind her ear, then tenderly skimmed his thumb along her jawline, adding to the chaos of feelings swirling inside her.

His eyes were caring as they met hers. "Okay," he said quietly, as if he understood what she couldn't explain, and then he reached out and gently pulled her into his arms and against his chest.

Ella didn't even resist. She flowed against him, closing her eyes and resting her cheek right were his heart beat strong and sure. He felt so good. So solid and warm, and everything about this moment made her wish that he could be hers. That nothing stood in the way of them being happy and *this* could be her life.

His hold around her tightened and he sighed into her hair. "I know that what's happening between us is unexpected. If someone would have told me ten days ago that I'd be standing in your bedroom with you in my arms, I would have called them insane. But here you are. Here *we* are, and I'm not ready to let you go just yet."

Her mind replayed the words *just yet*. As in,

he'd have to let her go eventually, which she already knew and accepted, even as gut-wrenching as the notion was. She just wasn't sure she'd be able to withstand the pain when he left . . . again.

She let her arms drift around his waist, let her hands slide up his strong, muscled back. "You shouldn't be here, Kyle," she whispered, not sure if she was trying to convince herself or him. Or if she was trying to protect her heart from the inevitable.

His fingers threaded through her hair, and he gently tugged her head back so she was looking up at him. A sexy smile teased the corner of his mouth, a clear intent to shift the mood *away* from the emotional stuff.

"Did you really think I was going to let you suck me off and not repay the favor?" he murmured, raising a dark brow.

A frisson of heat and awareness took up residence in the pit of her belly and made her nipples pucker tight—as if her body was battling against all the doubts and uncertainties filling her mind. "Kyle . . . "

"Tell me no, Sunshine," he murmured, ca-ressing the back of his hand along her cheek. "That's all you have to do. Say no, and I'll turn around and go. One simple word. You hold all the power, and the decision is yours. Tell me to leave. Do it."

She couldn't bring herself to say the word, because it went against everything she wanted and desired. She swallowed hard, praying she didn't regret her decision in the long run, though, given the choice, if she only had two months and a handful of weekends to spend with Kyle, even secretly, she'd take whatever she could—then figure out a way to move on without him after the building was done and he was gone.

He was waiting for her answer, the rigid set of his shoulders and the hope in his gaze belying the fact that he'd just told her he'd leave if that was her choice. Clearly, it wasn't what he wanted, either.

"Stay," she whispered, unable to stop the flood of honest emotions that spilled past her lips. "I can't stop wanting you, needing you, *aching* for you. It's constant, and I need it to go away. Make it go away, Kyle."

He shook his head as he grabbed the hem of her tank top and drew it up and over her head, revealing her breasts to his gaze. "I don't ever want it to go away," he said huskily, baring his own soul to her as he leaned down and kissed and nuzzled her neck. "I want you to always need me, ache for me . . ."

For now, in this moment, she could easily pretend that there would always be an *always*. She closed her eyes and moaned softly as he filled his big, warm hands with her breasts, then gasped when his mouth dipped down, closed over a taut, sensitive nipple, and sucked on the beaded tip. His fingers kneaded her flesh, his tongue swirled around an areola, and he gently guided her a few steps back, until her shoulders met the wall behind her.

This time, it was Kyle who dropped to his knees in front of her. He trailed hot, damp kisses down her stomach and rubbed his soft beard against her skin as he gripped the waistband of her sleep shorts and her panties and drew them both slowly, *oh so excruciatingly slowly*, over her hips, down her thighs, then let them drop to her feet.

She stepped out of the garments and Kyle tossed them aside, then sat back on his heels for a moment to trail his gaze up the length of her completely naked body, making her skin heat with anticipation. He hadn't even touched her yet and she could feel how wet she already was, how needy her pussy was for his lips, his fingers, his tongue.

"Fuck, you're beautiful," he murmured reverently, appreciatively, as he splayed his hands on her thighs and caressed them upward, until his thumbs reached her sex and he had her spread open to his hot, smoldering gaze.

"This, right here, is *mine*," he said on a low, possessive growl that thrilled her, then he buried his face between her legs and that thrill became an undeniable, breathtaking need.

Her head fell back against the wall and she moaned as she tipped her hips toward his mouth, giving him better access. He took full advantage, deepening the intimate kiss in ways she didn't even know was possible. Just as she'd been with him earlier, he was ruthless in his quest to make her come. His tongue was pure magic, and she clutched his hair in her hands as she started to shake, desperately needing something to hold on to as he rocked her world.

She wanted to scream and she was just barely coherent enough to remember that they weren't truly alone in the house. Instead, she bit down on her lower lip, holding back the cry of pleasure as the hot, demanding lick of his tongue turned greedy, ravenous, merciless, ultimately pushing her trembling and shuddering right over the precipice and straight into sheer bliss.

When she was finished bucking against his mouth, when the last of her internal tremors ebbed away, he stood up and braced his hands on her hips, giving her the support she needed to keep standing until she came to her senses again and her legs stopped shaking like jelly.

"I could do that all night long," he murmured wickedly. "But I'm dying to be inside you and feel you come around my cock, pulling me in and sucking my dick the same way your lips did earlier."

God, he was absolutely shameless. "You have the dirtiest mouth, *City Boy.*"

"You fucking love my filthy mouth," he said as he pulled his shirt over his head and dropped to the floor, the gleam in his eyes a little—*okay, a whole lot*—depraved. "The way it talks, the way it pleasures your pussy, the way it—"

She slapped her palm over his mouth and laughed softly, not sure she could take much more. "*Stop.*"

Pulling her hand away, he pressed the sweetest kiss in the center of her palm, contradicting his bold and brash statement. "Admit it."

She smiled and told him the truth. "I love your filthy, dirty mouth." *So much.*

He smirked triumphantly at her. "Yeah, you do. Now get up on the bed and spread your gorgeous legs for me, Sunshine, and show me what's mine."

Following his request, she climbed up onto the mattress and rested her head on a pillow, watching him at the foot of the bed as he stripped off the last of his clothes, then bent down and retrieved a condom from the pocket of his jeans. Before he could tear it open, she stopped him, and he tipped his head curiously at her.

"I'm on birth control," she assured him, pointing to the underside of her arm to indicate the implant embedded just under the skin. "I had it put in a few weeks before Tucker and I were supposed to get married because I thought it would be easier, but things ended between us before it went into effect . . . " She let the words trail off, and it didn't take him long to figure out what she was trying to say.

"We've *never* had sex without a condom," he said, his low, intimate voice reminding her of how he'd always driven to another town to buy protection because he hadn't wanted anyone to gossip about them, and there had been no way she would have gone to the local doctor for the pill, despite confidentiality laws. "In fact, if I'm being honest, I've never had sex with *anyone* without one."

She was glad. So, so glad. "Me, either," she whispered, trailing her fingers up the middle of her stomach as she gave him a come-hither smile. "Care to be my first? Again?" she teased.

Dropping the foil packet, he didn't hesitate to move up onto the bed. He grasped one of her ankles, then the other, widening her even more as he draped her legs over his thighs, took his cock in his hand, and dragged the head through the wetness between. "You're going to be my first again, too," he said, teasing them both with another slow, seductive stroke of his smooth, bare dick along her sensitive, needy flesh.

She moaned in frustration, her impatience and desire growing. "I want to feel every inch of you sliding into me, filling me, fucking me so hard and deep I won't know where I end and you begin."

"Jesus," he breathed as he finally positioned

the thick tip against her core, then braced his hands on either side of her shoulders, his dark eyes looking directly into hers as he grinned. "Who has the dirty, filthy mouth now?"

"Do it, Kyle," she begged, bending her knees back farther against his hips and gripping his ass in her hands to urge him forward. "Fuck me. Please."

He pushed his way into her in what felt like a long, endless stroke as his body settled completely over hers, both of them moaning at the exquisite sensation of having absolutely nothing between them. And then he started to move, gradually building the momentum into strong, hard, deep grunting lunges that awakened nerve endings inside her and had her nails digging urgently into the muscle and sinew along his back.

"You feel like fucking heaven." He bit the sensitive spot where her neck and shoulder joined, nipped her lobe, then kissed his way to her lips and devoured the soft, mewling moans she couldn't hold back.

She was completely surrounded by the man above her, deliciously pinned to the mattress by his weight as his thrusts gained force, their limbs tangled and entwined and her back arching wantonly so she could feel the friction of his chest rubbing against her aching nipples. His hands were in her hair, pulling her head to the side so he could fuse their mouths more deeply, so that they weren't connected just physically but intimately as well.

And emotionally. Oh, God, the longing swelling inside of her was almost painful, mixed in with the finest, most sublime rapture as her climax stole her breath and redefined the meaning of pleasure and euphoria.

And all she could do was let go and hope to God that when the time came, she'd survive the heartbreak he was bound to leave behind.

✧   ✧   ✧

ELLA LAY CURLED against Kyle's side, her cheek on his warm, solid chest and her hand on his flat stomach as he absently threaded his fingers through her hair in the shadowed bedroom. She was thoroughly sated and content for the moment to enjoy this quiet time with Kyle. In a few minutes, she was going to have to kick him out of her bed, because letting him spend the night wasn't a risk she was willing to take, not even if he promised to slip out at dawn. She knew he was heading back to the city in the morning, and already she was missing him since it would be another long week before she'd get to see him again.

You might as well get used to it, her mind taunted, because the terms of their affair weren't going to change any time soon, if ever.

"Ella . . ." Kyle's voice was deep and low and almost hesitant as it broke into her thoughts. "What happened between you and Tucker?"

She wasn't surprised he asked, considering how he'd reacted to seeing her ex-fiancé at the bar earlier, and as much as she didn't want to talk about Tucker right now, or ever, she wanted everything out in the open between them. No secrets. No misunderstandings. No resentments.

She exhaled a small breath. "What do you want to know?"

He absently wound a strand of hair around his finger. "Well, for starters, how did the two of you get involved in the first place?"

That was easy enough to answer. "We were always friends, but over time, that gradually changed. There's not a whole lot of available men in town, and Tucker was and is a good guy. Someone dependable that I always could count on, and I was . . . lonely," she forced herself to admit, because Kyle needed to know that, too. "When he asked me out on a date, I figured why not? What could it hurt?"

She felt Kyle's body tense slightly, but he'd been the one to ask about the relationship, and she wasn't going to lie about any of it to save his feelings. Besides, they'd already talked about the fact that he'd dated plenty of women in Chicago, even if they hadn't been long-term commitments.

"We had a nice time and he was easy to be with. It was . . . comfortable," she said, trying to find the right word to explain their dynamic.

A small, derisive laugh escaped him. "It sounds like you're talking about buying a couch for your living room. Nice, easy, comfortable."

She would have laughed, too, if he hadn't just nailed the painful truth. "That's just who Tucker is. He's not overtly sentimental or affectionate. He looks at things in a practical, sensible way, and I tend to be more . . ."

"Emotional?" he guessed.

The man knew her well. "Yes. And because of that, we could never really get past being *friends*. Not like us," she admitted, because despite putting Kyle in the friend zone, the chemistry and attraction between them had been too strong to deny. That had never been the case with Tucker.

"Yet you were going to marry him," he said gruffly, and she heard the hurt underlying his voice.

"Yes," she said quietly, and she wasn't proud of her reasons. "I *want* to be married. I want to share my life with someone, have a family with them, grow old together." Her throat grew tight because she'd always wanted, and had once envisioned, that kind of future for the two of them. "I don't want to be alone for the rest of my life, and I thought Tucker and I could make it work. Except, as time passed, I knew we'd never really get past being just friends. There was no passion in our relation-ship, nothing that excited or stimulated me mentally."

She swallowed hard and continued. "I knew in my heart that I wouldn't be happy married to him. And if I wasn't happy, we'd both be miserable. The last thing I'd ever want is to end up bitter and resentful because he couldn't give me what I needed, so I called off the wedding before we both made a huge mistake."

Kyle's hand drifted along her jaw, and he

tucked his thumb beneath her chin and raised her gaze to his. A frown furrowed his brow, and the look in his eyes was tentative. "Did you love him?"

It was a hard question to answer, because love came in all different forms, and when it came to Tucker, her sentiment had been based more on fondness, caring, and respect. Not the kind of intimacy and passion and excitement—and a dozen other wild, exhilarating emotions—that she felt when she was with Kyle.

"Of course I loved him," she replied honestly, not missing the flicker of pain that passed across his features, then was quickly gone. "I never would have agreed to marry Tucker if I didn't have feelings for him. But it was *never* the way I loved you," she said, unable to hold back that truth, too.

Her heart mocked her for using the word *love* in past tense, for taking the safe route, for giving in to her fears. She knew now that she'd never fallen *out* of love with Kyle, but she couldn't bring herself to say it out loud because she knew it wouldn't change anything between them, that their differences and lifestyles were too vast.

And sometimes, love just wasn't enough.

Chapter Eleven

Three months later . . .

KYLE LEANED BACK against the tailgate of his truck, his legs crossed at the ankles and his arms folded over his chest as he admired what he'd created for his mother in the past three months. The once dilapidated property had been transformed into a beautiful building, inside and out, that had the entire town excited about having a brand-new bakery and a venue for events . . . except, of course, Ella's father.

Kyle wasn't sure what Charles was more upset about. The fact that Kyle had purchased the building for his mother—which unfortunately resulted in Ella losing the opportunity to expand the market—or the events of the past that the bitter older man still judged him by and couldn't let go of.

At this point, Kyle was beginning not to care what the reasons were, except that it affected Ella's views on their relationship. Or rather, their secret affair, because that's exactly what it had been since the night they'd fallen back into bed together. Stolen moments on the weekends. Him sneaking into her bedroom—and sneaking right back out after their too short time together. Seeing her at the market while he worked on the building, yet maintaining their distance to keep any gossip at bay.

There were no fun, casual dates that normal couples went out on. No holding her hand and hanging out in public together. No, everything was reserved for those few hours they had together in her bedroom, and during the week, it was sporadic phone calls and texts that kept him going until the next time he could see her, be with her.

He fucking hated it. He'd played by Ella's rules, and on some level, he even understood why she was so guarded, that old habits died hard and for the past ten years, all she'd known was working at the market and taking care of her father. That had been her life because she'd been cast as the responsible one. The dependable one. And she clearly took the role seriously.

But something had to change, because they couldn't keep going on like this. And for the past three months, he'd been patient. He hadn't pushed her for more than she'd been willing to give, though he'd felt an undeniable shift between them over the course of that time, had seen and felt the evidence that there was more than just sex between them.

He already knew he was in love with Ella. Hell, he even understood that she was the reason he hadn't committed to any other woman in the past, because Ella gave him everything he needed. Everything he'd ever wanted. Except her love. Her heart was the one thing she'd kept under lock and key.

Then again, he hadn't said those three little words to her, either, mostly because he already knew how it would all play out. Instead of being overjoyed, she'd panic. Instead of jumping into his arms and declaring her love, as well, she'd push him away. He knew this because the few times he'd mentioned taking their relationship outside the bedroom, it hadn't gone well. Her doubts and fears had been immediate, and her fallback excuse was always the same: *You're going back to the city, where your life is, and I'm staying here, where I need to be for my father. A long-term, long-distance relationship isn't fair to either one of us.*

It always came back to that, and it was difficult to argue about her father and not come across as an insensitive asshole. But something had to give somewhere, and now that his time and work here in Woodmont were done, Kyle's biggest fear was that he was going to be the one Ella cut loose. Unless he did something about it. He just wished he knew what would or could change her mind.

With a sigh, he glanced over to the storefront for the bakery, smiling when he saw his mother bustling around inside. It hadn't taken her long to jump in and get involved and enjoy the prospect of being a business owner. She was a better decorator than she'd given herself credit for, because she'd gone with an awesome magical tea party theme inside the bakery with Alice in Wonderland elements, and everyone who glanced inside oohed and awed and couldn't wait until the place opened.

The industrial baking equipment he'd ordered would be delivered and installed that week, and every day, huge boxes of supplies and stock arrived, which kept his mother busy from morning until evening as she and the few other women she'd hired worked to put the place together for the grand opening that was happening in two weeks' time.

His gaze drifted to the main part of the building, which was over ten thousand square feet of venue space on its own, including a fully functional kitchen for catering. His mother had opted to go with a rustic, shabby-chic kind of look for the interior, and Kyle had to admit that he'd been more than a little leery when she'd used the word "shabby" to describe how she wanted to decorate the place—until he realized she meant *vintage*. Overall, the space had a pretty country vibe to it with just a touch of elegance, which suited the small town more than sophistication or glamour would have.

And then there was his secret project. A labor of love, literally. Over two thousand square feet devoted to Ella to make her dream come true. While his crew worked on the renovations for the venue and bakery, he'd spent his time in the sectioned-off area that was right up against the grocery store. Once the walls had gone up to split it off from the other part of the building, Kyle had spent most of his time creating all the shelves and displays that would allow her to expand to her heart's desire, and enable her to also help all the artisans in the area who wanted to get their merchandise into the hands of customers. The storefront was made of glass windows for shoppers to look inside, along with a separate door leading into the place. All that was left to do was break out a small section and install a large doorway that would connect the market to the new square footage, if that's what she wanted to do.

Surprisingly, she'd only asked him once what the space was for, and he'd been vague with his answer, telling her it was all part of the venue. She'd given him a slightly confused look because it seemed so out of place in comparison to the event center, but she hadn't questioned him again.

The object of his thoughts walked out of Fisher's Grocery, and much to his shock, she headed to where he was still leaning against the truck's tailgate. Very rarely did she seek him out on the weekends while he was working, so this was a rare and welcome treat.

She stopped a respectable distance away and gave him a warm smile. "I believe congratulations are in order," she said, as she glanced up at the CELEBRATIONS sign that had been installed earlier that morning.

Per his mother's request, the name of the venue and bakery had been engraved into a large piece of distressed wood. The old-style script had been painted a deep rose color, and the edges of the sign were outlined with an antique-looking moulding that tied it all together.

Ella looked back at him and pushed her fingers into the back pockets of her jeans when she should have been right next to his side, with his arm around her shoulder, as they looked at the new building *together*. That familiar frustration gnawed at him, but he didn't let it show. Not here and not now.

"The signage looks great, and the venue and bakery look phenomenal," she said, complimenting him. "You did good, City Boy. I think your mom is going to have a lot of success here."

"I hope so. Regardless, she'll be doing what she loves." Ella's words meant a lot to him, and he was grateful knowing that while he was working in the city, she'd be right next door if his mother needed help with something in a pinch.

That was one good thing that had come of him renovating the building. While Ella was reluctant to spend too much time around him while he was there, she had no issues talking to his mother or visiting Patricia while she was setting up the bakery or assisting her when there was something she needed a hand with. For his mother and Ella, at least, they'd rekindled that close bond they'd shared when he and Ella had been dating in high school.

"So, does this mean your work here is done?" There was a sadness in her voice, but a reluctant acceptance, too.

"With the venue and bakery, it is." With her, not so much. Not if he had his way.

But he knew this wasn't the time or place to have that discussion. Instead, he decided it was time to make Ella's dream a reality. "I have something for you," he said, pushing away from the tailgate. "Hang on while I get it."

She tipped her head curiously, causing the tail of her braid to swish over her shoulder. "Okay."

He rounded the truck, opened the passenger door, and retrieved the small square box he'd tucked into the glove box before leaving the city on Friday night. Daphne had helped him out with the presentation, insisting that the small white box needed a bow for some flourish, and she'd tied a big, fat pink ribbon around it. Kyle had to admit it looked pretty, and he was glad that Daphne had given it a woman's touch.

He returned to where Ella was still standing, her gaze more than a little wary as she glanced at the gift he held out to her. She didn't take it, and instead her eyes jumped up to his, wide and hesitant.

"What's this?" she asked, her hands still jammed into the back pockets of her jeans.

"It's exactly what it looks like," he said with an encouraging smile. "It's a gift for you. Something I want you to have because you deserve it and I want you to be happy."

Tentatively, she finally accepted the present, and a sudden bout of nerves and anticipation flip-flopped in his stomach as he watched her unravel the ribbon, then lift the lid.

Confusion etched her expression as she glanced from the item in the box to him. "A key? For what?"

"Turn around and look at the building, Ella," he coaxed softly, relieved when she did as he asked, even though her bewilderment was still apparent. "Remember when you asked me what that space on the left was for? The one right next to the market with its own separate door?"

"Yes. It's part of the event center," she said, still not connecting the dots.

"No, it's yours, Sunshine," he said gently.

Her breath hitched in her throat as she turned her head his way, those beautiful green eyes filled with the slightest bit of hope. "What do you mean, *mine?*"

"I built it for you." It took every ounce of willpower he had not to touch her in that moment like he ached to. "It's yours, to do with as you please."

"What?" She shook her head in shock. "No, I can't just *take* it."

He smiled, because he'd anticipated that re-action and had a ready response. "You're not taking it. I'm *giving* it to you. As a gift. And that key fits into the front door. Unfortunately, I'm not able to put just that one section into your name because the property can't be split up that way, but it's all yours. Not your father's. *Yours,*" he stressed, then added, "No strings attached." It was important that she knew, that, too. The store didn't come with conditions and whether or not things worked out with them had no bearing on it.

Her eyes shone with awe and tears he wasn't

sure how to interpret. "You honest-to-God built that for me?" she asked in disbelief.

He'd build her a hundred of them if it meant he could see that happy look in her eyes every single day. "I honest-to-God did. And now that you have it, I can make that store so it connects directly to the market or leave it as a separate storefront. The choice is yours."

"I don't even know what to say," she whispered as she hugged the box and key to her chest. "Thank you doesn't seem adequate."

"You're welcome," he said, realizing how different this all should have been.

Instead of her hiding her excitement because they were a secret, he should have been picking her up in his arms and spinning her around while she squealed with joy. He should have been kissing her long and hard in front of anyone who was watching before rushing her over to the store so they could start making plans for the future together.

Problem was, he wasn't sure where their future stood.

Right now, he understood that she was overwhelmed. That she needed time to process what had just happened and wrap her mind around the gift he'd given her. And he also knew she needed time to figure out how to tell her father that Kyle had built a storefront for her. He didn't like it, but he couldn't change it, either.

"Are you coming over tonight?" she asked, her happiness subdued for now.

"Yes." But not for what she was insinuating. In her mind, she was probably thinking of all the ways she could show her appreciation, but sex wasn't what he wanted. It wasn't what his *heart* wanted. It wanted answers and reassurances and far more than just another night in her bed.

He wanted forever, and he had no idea if Ella was capable of giving him what he needed. But this time, he'd be the one issuing the ultimatum.

All of her or nothing at all.

✧　✧　✧

FOR THE VERY last time, Kyle crawled through Ella's bedroom window a little after ten, when her father was normally in bed for the evening. The next time he came to see Ella, *if* there was one after their conversation tonight, he'd be walking through the front door like a normal guy who was dating her would. Or he'd never step foot into this house again. The decision was up to her, and the fate of their future was in her hands.

She was standing in the middle of the room, anxiously waiting for him, bouncing from foot to foot like an excited little kid. As soon as he cleared the window and the curtain fell back in place, she flung her hands around his neck. She jumped up into his arms, her legs wrapped enthusiastically around his waist as her mouth landed on his—exactly how her reaction *should* have been when he'd given her the key to her new storefront earlier today.

With his hands holding her ass to help keep her from sliding down his body, he let Ella kiss him, because he wasn't sure if this would be the last chance he'd get to taste her. Her mouth was soft and warm, her lips sliding and melding against his like a perfect dream. It was a kiss of gratitude and appreciation, with an underlying trace of seduction. She moaned so sweetly when she finally lifted her head again, and he let go of her butt so she could stand on her own two feet.

She touched her palm to his cheek, her fingers sensually caressing the short beard covering his jaw. "Kyle," she whispered so reverently it made him ache deep inside. "I still can't believe that storefront is all mine."

"Did you tell your father?" It was a question he had to ask, and the storefront certainly wasn't something she'd be able to hide from her father for long.

She bit her bottom lip, the shine from her gaze dimming with uncertainty. "Not yet. I'm figuring out how to tell him so he doesn't have another stroke," she muttered, glancing away.

He wasn't sure if she was being facetious or not, but when it boiled right down to the heart of the matter, the fact that she was delaying her own happiness to accommodate her father just didn't bode well for them as a couple. At some point, she had to stand up to her father, for herself. For them.

With his stomach in knots, he grabbed her hands and pulled them away so she was no longer touching him, because he couldn't think straight otherwise. "Ella . . . we need to talk."

She swallowed hard, as if knowing where this conversation was headed, though she didn't say a word. But the wariness in her gaze, mixed in with a dose of fear, spoke for itself.

"I can't keep doing this, Ella. *We* can't keep doing this," he said, getting right to the point.

"This?" she asked, her voice strained, even as she hedged with her reply to avoid the inevitable.

"Being a secret from everyone, and especially from your father. Only seeing you a few hours every weekend here in your bedroom." That familiar frustration rose up again, and he pushed his fingers through his hair, forcing himself to keep calm. "I've spent three months accepting whatever you were willing to give to this thing between us . . . but it's not enough."

Her fingers fluttered anxiously up to her throat, her eyes big and filled with dismay. "It has to be enough for now."

"*For now?*" he repeated, his tone rising incredulously as he jammed his hands on his hips. "And when does that end, Ella? When does *for now* become something more than me crawling through your window for a quick fuck?" His words were crude, but he was starting to feel desperate, like the best thing that had ever happened to him was slipping through his fingers for the second time in his life. "When will I be able to take you out on a date like normal couples do? When can we start building toward some kind of future together?"

"What if we can't have a future together?"

she demanded, her voice suddenly thick with tears. "Are you forgetting that I live here in Woodmont, and you live in the city, which I hate? But that's where your job is. That's where your life is and has been for the past ten years. And this is where my life will always be."

Despite his anger at the situation, he understood her concerns. "We'll figure it out, but we can't even do that because our relationship hasn't extended outside of the fucking bedroom."

"That's because there isn't anything to figure out," she nearly yelled at him.

"I love you, Ella." The words came tumbling out, and it nearly gutted him when he saw the pain in her eyes, when he didn't hear the same response from her lips even though he *knew* she had to feel the same. "For ten long years, I've felt so empty inside, waiting to feel something again for another woman, and it never happened and you want to know why? Because *you* are the one, Ella. You will always be the one. Doesn't that count for something? Anything?"

"I don't know," she said, squeezing her eyes shut for a moment, her voice conflicted and confused. "I don't know."

"I want you in my life." He couldn't be more open and honest and straight-forward about that.

"*This* is my life," she said, waving a hand in the air around her to indicate where she was and who she was with and where she would stay.

"No, this is the life you *think* you need to lead," he said more firmly. "Out of a sense of obligation to your father. Because your sister isn't around to help and you feel like it's all on you to shoulder everything at the expense of your own happiness. What about you, Ella? What about what *you* want? What about your life and your future? When does any of that matter?"

She never had the opportunity to answer, because the rattling of the doorknob, then a loud knock on the door made them both freeze in place at the sudden interruption.

"Ella?" her father said from the other side, his voice gruff. "Who's in your room with you and why is your door jammed shut?"

The panic that passed across Ella's features was instantaneous. "No one's here, Dad," she said, holding Kyle's gaze with a plea in her own for him to remain quiet.

"Ella, I heard loud voices. One distinctly male," her father insisted, giving the door another push, but the stopper beneath the bottom made it impossible for him to get inside. "What's going on in there?"

Ella never broke eye contact with Kyle. "Nothing," she replied, forcing an airy quality to her voice that didn't ring true, no matter how hard she was trying. "I'm just getting ready for bed."

Kyle actually found irony in this moment. Three months of sneaking into this house to spend time with Ella, and tonight of all nights her father discovered them together. He hated Ella's denial, that she was driven by fear, and he realized he had two choices. He could give in to the silent request in her eyes and slip back out the window like he'd never been here so she could open the door and prove to father that she was alone, or Kyle could confront the past that stood between them.

It didn't take him long to make his decision. He started for the bedroom door.

"Kyle," she hissed in a frantic voice, but he didn't stop his approach.

Reaching the only thing separating himself from Ella's father, Kyle kicked the rubber wedge out from under the door, then pulled it open. Charles gasped and took a step back as he stared at Kyle in shock.

"What are you doing here?" Charles demanded.

"I'm here for your daughter," Kyle said calmly, even as he felt Ella right behind him, her anxiety nearly palpable. "I'm here because I love her," he went on, despite the flush of rage spreading across the other man's face. "I'm here because I want her in my life."

"You don't deserve my daughter," Charles said, his features twisting with bitterness and resentment. "Your family is responsible for everything *this* family has suffered!"

"Dad, please," Ella said, trying to calm down her father. "Don't do this."

Charles started breathing hard, his chest rising and falling more rapidly. "It's true, and I don't want you anywhere near Ella. Ever."

Kyle's jaw clenched in anger. He was done with being condemned for his brother's sins, for his father's actions. For being accused of something he'd had no part of. "The only two people in my family who are to blame for anything, are my father and my brother. But mostly Todd, because what he did to Gwen was a really shitty thing and unforgiveable. But my mother has done nothing to deserve your contempt, and as for me, the only thing I'm guilty of is loving and caring for Ella. Back then *and* now."

The older man pointed a stern finger at Kyle. "Stay . . . away . . . from my daughter," Charles huffed, then grabbed at his chest as he stumbled backward.

"Dad!" Ella called out in alarm.

Shit, was the guy having another stroke? Instinctively, Kyle reached out and caught the man's arm before he could hit the wall, and in the next instant, Ella was next to her father, tucking herself under Charles' arm and guiding him down the hallway to the living room.

"Dad, you need to take deep breaths," she said, her voice quivering with worry and fear, even as she took control of the situation.

"I want him out of my house," Charles wheezed as Ella sat him down in a leather recliner, then she pulled a drawer open on the end table and retrieved a bottle of pills.

Kyle had no idea what was going on, and despite the older man's insistent orders for him to get out, Kyle wasn't about to leave until he knew everything was okay. "Let me call the paramedics," he said, reaching into his pocket for his cell phone.

"He'll be fine," Ella snapped at him, stopping Kyle before he could connect the call to 911. "He's not having a stroke. He's having an anxiety attack. He'll be okay once he calms down."

From Kyle's perspective, it looked equally bad, and he couldn't stop the twinge of guilt for pushing the man to his breaking point. "What can I do to help?"

"Nothing," she said, her voice as flat as the look in her eyes as she assisted her father in taking his meds. "You can't be here, Kyle. You need to go. Now."

Everything inside of Kyle went ice-cold, her words taking him straight back to the night when he'd lost Ella the first time, and the similar demand she'd made then, too: *The only thing I want right now is for you to get out of my life.*

The only thing missing was a slap to his face.

Without another word, he walked out the front door. He headed back to his mother's, picked up the duffel bag of belongings he'd brought with him for the weekend, gave his mom a quick explanation of what had happened, then drove to his condo in the city.

Ella had made her choice, and it wasn't him.

Chapter Twelve

HE WASN'T COMING back.

Almost a week later, the realization still hurt Ella's heart as she stood inside of the beautiful new store that Kyle had not only built for her but had selflessly given to her. All because he wanted her to be happy. To have something that was her very own.

She couldn't have been more miserable and devastated. The constant heartache was so bad she couldn't even bring herself to go forward with her plans to call all the artisans in the area to bring in their merchandise to fill up the displays and shelves, because none of this meant anything to Ella if she didn't have that one certain person to share the joys and successes with.

No, she'd royally screwed up any chance of a future she could have had with Kyle. She'd let her father influence her choices once again, and she'd lost the one man who knew her so well. The only man who'd cared deeply for her, protected her, loved her unconditionally, and had given her so much without getting anything in return. Or at least not what he deserved—her love.

And she did love Kyle. So much it was painful to breathe knowing she might not ever see him again. That she'd have to live the rest of her life knowing that he'd come to the conclusion that she wasn't worth the hassle, because for the second time in ten years, she'd pushed him away when things had gotten rough, instead of leaning on him and trusting him with her heart.

And now, she was alone. Again.

"You know, Kyle would want you to put this store to good use instead of leaving it empty."

Ella jumped at the sound of Patricia Coleman's voice behind her, and she turned around, not all that surprised to see Kyle's mother standing there in a frilly pink baking apron, her gaze both kind and sympathetic. The other woman had been crazy busy getting ready for her big grand opening, and the fact that she'd taken the time to come and check on Ella spoke to the kind of thoughtful woman she was—a trait that her younger son had emulated.

"How could something I've always wanted and dreamed of be such a painful reminder of everything I've lost?" Her voice was tight and scratchy from all her late-night crying jags, when the impact of what she'd done hit her hard.

Patricia moved into the store and closer to Ella. "Honey, it doesn't have to be that way."

Ella gave the other woman a sad smile. "Well, I'm not sure that Kyle can forgive me for what I did and what I said." The devastation on his face when she'd told him to leave her house after her father's anxiety attack was something she'd never be able to erase from her mind.

"Oh, I think you'd be surprised," Patricia said, absently smoothing her hand over the apron she was wearing. "That boy of mine has a heart as big as this state, and I know he's crazy about you. He always has been. And still is."

A lump rose in Ella's throat, because she felt the same way about Kyle. Without a doubt, that man was her soul mate. The one person who knew her inside and out and loved her anyway. He was her other half that had been missing for ten long years, and the thought of going through the rest of her life without him was pure agony.

"Last Saturday night, before he left to go back to the city, he told me to look after you," Patricia said, gently placing her hand on Ella's arm. "He wanted to make sure that you were okay after everything that had happened. But I know you're not. You look as heartbroken as he sounds when I talk to him on the phone. You two belong together. You always have and you always will. Some things are just meant to be."

Ella laughed derisively. "Trying tell that to my father."

"I would if you'd let me," Patricia said, her eyes sparkling mischievously before she turned serious once again. "I think some people find it easier to hold on to anger and resentments instead of letting them go, and a lot of people suffer for that, including you and Kyle. I also think that maybe your father just needs some-one to blame for Gwen's . . . behavior," she said, being polite about the reputation Ella's sister had around town, "and what happened with her pregnancy and miscarriage."

Gwen certainly hadn't been an angel in that situation, but the one thing Ella had learned over the years was that her father refused to think of Gwen as, well, the slut she'd been— and still was. It was a painful pill for any father to swallow or accept, and even now, he still wanted to believe that Gwen was just misunderstood.

Ella glanced around the store once again, worrying on her bottom lip. There were other doubts and worries she had when it came to her and Kyle, and because Patricia was the closest thing to a mother that she'd had in a long time, and also because she knew Kyle so well, she expressed one of her concerns.

"I'm not sure how a long-distance relationship is going to work between us," she said honestly as she looked back at the other woman. "I live and work here, and now I'm starting a new store. He lives and works in Chicago. It's not an easy fix. Did he tell you that I went to visit him in the city to talk to him about the building and had a full-blown panic attack because of how closed-in and loud everything was?"

"He did," she said with a little laugh. "But there is one thing I know that is true. Kyle has never had a reason *not* to live in the city. He works in Chicago so it's convenient, but that doesn't mean he's not willing to compromise for someone he loves. *You're* his reason, Ella. He would do anything to have a life with you."

The word *compromise* was like a huge light bulb moment for Ella. Give and take. Meeting him halfway, someway, somehow. He'd given her three months of being patient and understanding, and when push came to shove, she'd shoved him right out of her life without giving them a chance to *figure it out*. That's all he'd asked for . . . time to figure out a solution to make things work between them. Because he loved her and because *she would always be the one.*

She placed a hand on her rapidly beating heart as his words came back to her, so raw and honest and true. It was everything she felt for him in return, and she had to tell him, because he would always be the man she loved and wanted to spend the rest of her life with. And in order to do that, she had to be willing to make sacrifices on her end to be with him, even if that meant somehow splitting time between Woodmont and Chicago, or somewhere in between.

A small frisson of hope swelled through her.

She could do this. For Kyle. For them. It was a Friday evening, the very worst time for her to drive into the city, but she couldn't go another day without him in her life. Or without him knowing just how much she loved him.

"I have to go," she said to Patricia in a rush of breath.

The other woman just smiled knowingly, and while she went back to finish setting up the bakery next door for the grand opening in a week, Ella locked up the shop that Kyle had given her and went home to change.

When she walked through the front door, her father was sitting in his leather recliner watching the news, while Betsy was on the couch quietly knitting. Her dad had been giving her the silent treatment all week long, and today was no different. It was as if he was punishing her for being with Kyle, and as she headed into her bedroom to strip out of her grocery attire to take a quick shower, she realized that her father's attitude was *his* issue, not hers. Not anymore.

Twenty minutes later, wearing a pretty dress and a pair of heels, with her hair down and a hint of makeup on, she made her way back to the front door without a word.

"Where are you going?" her father asked gruffly.

Taking a deep breath, Ella stopped and turned to face him. Out of the corner of her eye, she saw Betsy's knitting needles come to a stop as the other woman no doubt wanted to witness what was about to happen. At least Ella knew she had an ally in Betsy, that she'd be there to calm Charles down after the conversation Ella knew they were going to have. Because it was a long time coming, and her father needed to understand that there was absolutely nothing he could say or do that would stop her from being with Kyle this time around.

She lifted her chin fearlessly, because that's exactly how she felt—confident and self-assured in who she was and what she wanted. "I'm going into the city to see Kyle," she said.

Her father's dark brows pinched together in disapproval. "Ella—"

"Stop," she said, cutting off her father because it didn't matter what he had to say to her. It was more important that he heard what she needed to say to him. "I'm not asking for your permission, and I don't need your approval. I'm almost twenty-eight years old, and this is my decision, not yours. I've given up the past ten years taking care of you and running the market, and it's my turn to live my life and be happy. And I'm the happiest when I'm with Kyle."

Her father's face had turned red in anger, and while she knew this might induce another anxiety attack, he had his pills and he had Betsy and she trusted the other woman to take care of him. "I'm not sure why Gwen has gotten a free pass all these years for her behavior, because she's far from perfect. No one *forced* her to sleep with Todd back then, and while I agree that Todd should have stepped up and been a man about the situation, Gwen is not faultless. If she cared about you, about us, she'd be here right now, instead of with some random guy she met one weekend. She's always been selfish and self-centered, and I don't see that changing anytime soon."

She could see her father's chest rising and falling quickly, and it wasn't easy for Ella not to rush to his side like she normally would have. In fact, it was damn hard to stay where she was, but a quick glance at Betsy, who gave her an encouraging nod, told her that the other woman knew Charles wasn't in danger of having a stroke. Ella recalled the conversation she'd had with Betsy a short while ago—*for a long time now*

I've suspected that he acts frail and incapable because you've always catered to him. He won't wither away if you go out and live your life.

Ella hadn't been in the frame of mind three months ago to take Betsy's words to heart or to act on them, but she realized that, yes, she'd catered to her father's behavior—enabled him, even—for way too long.

"So, yes, I'm going to the city to be with Kyle," she reiterated. "And if everything goes the way I'm hoping, I won't be back tonight. Hell, I might not be back all weekend, and William is more than capable of taking care of the store while I'm gone. Have a good night, Dad."

Her father gaped at her as she finished walking to the door, opened it, and stepped out onto the porch. She closed the door behind her and stopped for a moment to just *breathe*.

"I need my goddamn pills!" Ella heard her father yell from inside the house.

"Charles, you need to calm down and stop being so ornery," Betsy replied in that no-nonsense voice of hers. "Let that girl go live her life and stop meddling in it."

The two of them continued to bicker, and Ella laughed softly and shook her head as she made her way to her car, knowing she was leaving her dad in good hands. There was no doubt in her mind that her relationship with her father might be strained for a while, but she also knew he'd never disown her. And maybe, hopefully, given time, he'd come to realize and accept that Kyle was the best thing that had ever happened to her.

Feeling as though a hundred-pound weight had been lifted off her shoulders, she got into her car and started the two hour-long drive into the city to get her man.

✧　✧　✧

FRESHLY SHOWERED AND wearing an old, comfortable pair of sweat pants, Kyle sat in an armchair facing the windows overlooking the twinkling lights on Lake Michigan as he took a drink of the Jack Daniel's Tennessee Whiskey he'd poured himself. He wasn't a big drinker. A beer here and there with friends, but knowing he was heading into his first long weekend without Ella, he'd opted for something more fortifying.

Every day this past week, he'd held out hope that he'd hear from her. A phone call. A text. Anything at all to give him some kind of

indication that maybe she'd come to the realization that he was worth fighting for. That *they*
were worth fighting for.

That he hadn't royally fucked everything up
by walking away from her.

No, as much as he hated the way things had
ended between them, he knew he'd done the
right thing by leaving, because he couldn't go
another three months, or longer, hiding a
relationship with Ella. And it didn't even matter
that he'd come up with a possible solution to
their distance issue. If she didn't stand up to her
father and resolve *those* issues, they had no
chance at a future together. End of story. And
apparently, end of them.

He downed another gulp of whiskey, welcoming the burn that slid down his throat and
settled in his belly. Then he went ahead and
finished off the last of the shot. Drowning his
sorrows was beginning to sound like a damn
fine idea.

He pushed out of his chair to go and refill
his glass just as one of the intercoms on the wall
buzzed from the doorman downstairs. Kyle
couldn't imagine what the guy could want, and
he was interrupting Kyle's pity party, but he
went ahead and pressed the button and an-

swered with a curt, "Yes?"

"There's an Ella Fisher here to see you," the older gentleman said. "Would you like for me to let her up?"

Kyle frowned. For a moment, he thought he was hearing things. Ella was here, in the city, on a Friday night? Considering her aversion to Chicago, that didn't seem likely . . .

"Sir?" the doorman prompted. "Ms. Fisher said it was important that she speak with you. What would you like me to do?"

Cautious optimism surged though Kyle, and he replied before Ella took his silence for a *no*. "Yes, let her up, please."

The line disconnected, and it seemed like it took forever to hear a knock on his door while he paced the entryway. He opened the door, and there she was, looking like the bright ray of sunshine that he called her. A frazzled-looking ray of sunshine, but *his* nonetheless. He hoped.

"Umm, can I come in?" she asked tentatively.

"Of course." He stepped back and she brushed past him as she walked inside his place and into the living room. He followed behind, and the sweet scent of lemons filled his senses, instinctively stirring his desire for her. Then again, everything about this woman made him feel like a lovesick fool around her.

She turned around to face him. From the dress she had on to her gorgeous hair falling around her shoulders to the blatant fortitude in her eyes as she met his gaze, she looked absolutely stunning wearing all that confidence. It stole his breath and made his heart pound wildly in his chest because of what it could mean.

He still found it hard to believe that she'd braved the city to come to him. "What are you doing here?"

She lifted her chin a notch, and the sudden fire in her eyes told him that she was prepared to fight for what she wanted. "I'm here to tell you that I love you, which is something I should have said a week ago. Because it's true. I never stopped loving you," she said, a vulnerable tremor in her voice. "And I can't imagine my life or my future without you in it."

His relief was so overwhelming he nearly dropped to his knees in gratitude. He wanted to take her in his arms and hold her forever, but there was just enough wariness still left in him to address the biggest conflict that stood between them. "What about your father?"

"Well . . . I don't care what my father thinks, because this is my life and my choice, and I told him so. Is he happy that I'm here? Absolutely not," she said with a soft, derisive laugh. "But I'm the happiest I've ever been when I'm with you, wherever that may be. And if that means we need to compromise and split our time between Chicago and Woodmont"—she exhaled a deep breath—"I'll somehow learn to deal with getting around in the city. I'll do anything to be with you, Kyle, because what we have is worth it, and I'm not giving you up a second time."

The fact that she was willing to make that sacrifice for him, *for them*, told him everything he needed to know. That she was committed to making this work, that she was willing to face the obstacles, that in the end, it was about the choices they made together.

He moved toward her, finally closing the distance between them because he needed to touch her so badly. When they were standing toe-to-toe, he picked up her hands and held them in his. She lifted her gaze to his, and the emotion there and the love for him shining in the depths nearly slayed his heart.

He raised his palms to her face, and, unable

to stop himself from taking what he absolutely needed more than his next breath, he lowered his head to hers and kissed her—slow and sweet and infinitely tender. Telling her without words what she meant to him, that she alone made his world complete. She was his shining light, his north star that would always guide him home.

He finally ended the kiss, a soft, dreamy look in her eyes. "God, I love you, Ella Fisher."

She smiled, her expression radiant. "I love you, too. So much."

He skimmed his thumbs along her smooth cheeks. "But I'm not letting you move to the city."

The happiness and exhilaration in her gaze dimmed, and he realized she'd mistaken his words for a rejection. Ahhh, far from it.

He quickly corrected her wrong assumption. "I appreciate all the concessions you're willing to make for us, but this past week has given me a lot of time to think about logistics. Yes, my job and company are in the city, but my hours are completely flexible. We can live near or in Woodmont and you'd be close to the market, and I can make that one-hour commute. People do it all the time."

She leaned into him, her hands pressing flat against his bare chest. "Are you absolutely sure?"

"Positively sure. We'll make it work. I promise, because there is no way in hell I want to go through another week like I just had without you." He gently brushed back a strand of hair from her face, letting his touch linger. "I'll keep my condo, and we can use it if we ever need to stay in the city—" She grimaced at that and he laughed. "Or if I'm working a late night and need a place to crash. But I really don't think that will be likely, because the only place I want to be every single night is in bed, right next to you, so I can wake up every morning to the most beautiful woman on the planet. So, maybe I'll just sell the condo."

She skimmed her hands up to his shoulders and around his neck. "We'll figure it out, together," she said, pulling his head down to hers for another kiss.

"Yeah, together," he reiterated against her soft, parted lips before losing himself in the delicious taste of her. Until he was absolutely insane with the need to get inside of her again.

He lifted her in his arms, and she squealed at being literally swept off her feet as he carried her to his bedroom.

After a moment, she relaxed and sighed as she trailed one of her hands along his shoulder and down his arm to squeeze his bicep. "It's a good thing you're well built, City Boy."

"I'm also built to last, baby," he said, meaningfully. He was a forever kind of guy.

"Yeah, you are," she agreed appreciatively as he set her down on her heels at the foot of his bed.

She turned around so he could unzip her dress, and he placed hot, damp kisses along the skin he exposed, making her shiver. "You know what all this means, don't you?"

"That I'm about to get laid by the sexiest guy in Chicago?" she mused seductively.

"Yeah, that, too." He chuckled as he pushed the dress off her shoulders and it fell to the floor at her feet, leaving her in a lacy pair of panties, a matching bra, and those hot-as-fuck heels.

His dick strained against the front of his sweat pants, begging to be let out, but he ignored the demand. He wanted to strip Ella bare before he got naked himself. He unclipped the back of her bra, let it join her dress on the ground, then walked around her until they were face-to-face and he could fill both of his hands with her soft, full breasts before dipping his head to take a tight nipple into his mouth.

"It means all this compromise we're both going to be making . . ." He kissed his way down her stomach and pushed his fingers into the waistband of her panties to drag them down her hips. "We're going to have to get married."

Her breath hitched noticeably. "Yeah?" she asked softly, hopefully.

"Yep." With her underwear gone, he straightened again so he was looking into her beautiful eyes as he guided her back toward the bed, still wearing the fuck-me shoes—he thoroughly intended to do just that. Numerous times and a dozen different positions. "No living in sin for us."

She laughed out loud at that as she scooted up the mattress, until she was lying against the pillows on her back, looking like a temptress, while he quickly stripped off his sweat pants.

"We've been sinning for the past three months," she said in amusement as she deliberately spread her legs, showing him how wet she already was for him. How needy. "We're about to sin right now," she teased him.

"Fuck yeah, we are," he said huskily as he

dove between her legs to eat her up, the hungry, greedy slide of his lips and tongue adding to their plethora of dirty, filthy sins.

She gasped in shock, then moaned in pleasure, and eventually, she twisted her fingers in his hair, shamelessly rode his mouth, and cried out his name as she came gloriously, furiously hard against the flick and glide of his tongue.

Before she had a chance to recover, and while her pussy was still fluttering from the remnants of her blissful orgasm, he moved up and completely over her body, then buried himself balls deep inside her with one long, fluid stroke. She arched up against him, wrapped those long legs around his waist, and he felt the erotic dig of those heels scraping across his skin and wreaking havoc with his self-control.

He tried not to move, not until they cleared up one more thing. Shoving his hands into her hair, he tipped her head back so she had no choice but to meet his gaze. Her eyes were dilated, dark with desire, and he smiled down at her, because she was so perfect, and everything he'd ever wanted and needed in his life.

"You distracted me with all that sinning," he murmured deeply, wickedly. "And I forgot to ask you something very important, because I don't want to make any assumptions."

She licked her bottom lip and tried to squirm beneath him to make him move, and ended up making a frustrated sound when he held still. "Yeah, and what's that?" she asked impatiently.

"A formal proposal," he said, and instantly felt her go soft beneath him, her eyes wide with awe and love and a hundred other emotions he completely understood, because he felt the same. "Ella Fisher, will you marry me?"

She didn't even hesitate with her answer. "I will, City Boy," she said, happy tears of pure delight shimmering in her eyes. "I can't wait to finally be Mrs. Kyle Coleman."

And he couldn't wait to make her completely and utterly his.

Epilogue

Six months later . . .

KYLE HELD HIS beautiful bride in his arms as they swayed to their first dance as husband and wife. Her hair was swept away from her gorgeous face and piled on top of her head in loose curls, baby's breath, and pearl clips, while the rest cascaded down her back in soft waves, just how he liked it best. Her dress was vintage lace, the style more romantic than overtly sexy, but he loved the sensual way the cut of the fabric skimmed the curves of her body.

As she looked up at him, he felt his heart swell in his chest. With the shine of true love in her eyes, the radiant glow of contentment on her face, and the pure happiness that radiated from the smile on her lips, she was absolutely stunning.

Damn, he was the luckiest man alive, and to think this was just the beginning of their long and amazing future as a wedded couple. They had years to love each other, to build a family together, and to make their lives everything they dreamed it would ever be.

Today, as they'd spoken their vows, they'd been surrounded by friends and family. It had been a perfect sunny day for an outdoor ceremony, and their reception was being held at Celebrations—the first wedding reception his mother's new venue had hosted. And even though Kyle had told his mom to be a guest at the reception—and not the owner of the place—she couldn't help but fuss over the food, the cake, and the decor. It made her feel useful and joyful, so Kyle let her do her thing. He was all about making the women in his life happy.

The past six months had been busy ones. He and Ella had found a small place to rent on the outskirts of town until they found exactly what they wanted to buy—though, admittedly, he'd purposely stalled purchasing a house, using the excuse that they'd have more time after the wedding to give the search more of their focus and attention. But the drive into Chicago wasn't horrible, and he'd adapted his hours to miss rush-hour traffic to and from the city. He never stayed at his condo, and had recently put it on the market to sell.

Ella had named her storefront the Artisan Marketplace, and in the few short months that she'd opened the doors, the place was already profitable and growing weekly with new products for customers. She'd made the decision not to connect it to her father's grocery store, leaving it as her own separate space. Just last week, she'd talked to her dad about selling Fisher's Grocery, because she wanted to focus solely on expanding her business. Surprisingly, her father hadn't balked at the idea and saw it as a way to invest the money to fund his retirement, and even some traveling, too, with Betsy—the woman who was now living with him, not as a caretaker but as his significant other.

Yes, Ella and her father had managed to resolve their differences. It had taken time, *lots of time*, but once Charles realized that Ella was going to marry Kyle no matter how he felt about it, he'd begrudgingly come around. Kyle had a feeling that Betsy had something to do with that shift in attitude, but it didn't really matter who or how it had happened, just that it had. Even Charles' animosity toward Kyle had gradually diminished, and again, it didn't matter how or why, because it made Ella happy that the two men in *her* life could coexist peacefully.

As the song ended, someone tapped Kyle on his arm, and he turned to find the object of his thoughts standing there. Charles looked incredibly handsome in his black suit, and he'd been so proud to walk his daughter down the aisle. There had been tears in the old man's eyes, though his voice had been gruff when he'd told Kyle to *take care of his baby*.

"Mind if I have a dance with my daughter?" Charles asked, and Kyle wasn't going to refuse that bonding moment between the two of them.

Kyle lifted his wife's hand—God, he loved being able to call her his wife—and placed a tender kiss on her knuckles that earned him a smile. "I'll be back soon," he promised, then handed her over to her father so they could have some time alone.

He made his way to where his friend Connor Prescott was standing off to the side by himself, watching everyone else while he sipped a drink he'd gotten from the open bar.

"Congratulations, man," Connor said, slapping him on the back. "I'm really happy for you, but I have to admit that I'm starting to feel like the odd man out."

There was humor in his friend's voice, but also a note of truth, too, and Kyle understood why when he glanced out at the guests at his reception and saw all the pairings through Connor's eyes. Everyone around him was getting domesticated. First, there'd been Wes and Natalie—Connor's good friend and his little sister—then Max, who'd found love with a matchmaker, of all things. Their two partners were beyond happy as husbands, and both Natalie and Max's wife, Hailey, were even a few months pregnant at the same time—and Kyle was eager to start on a family with Ella, as well.

Even Claire and Nolan were paired off, and Kyle wouldn't be surprised if there was an engagement between the two of them fairly soon since they'd become so inseparable.

But there was one thing that Kyle knew to be true. Love was an unpredictable thing. You never knew when it was going to happen, or how, or with whom. A year ago, Kyle never would have envisioned his life with Ella after what had happened between them ten years ago, but here he was, married to his very best friend.

He glanced at Connor and imparted the best advice he could. "When you least expect it, it's gonna happen, so don't worry about being an old maid just yet," he said with a laugh.

Connor chuckled, too. "Maybe I should feel lucky that I've dodged the matrimonial bullet."

The bride and groom stayed at the reception for another two hours. They danced, they mingled, they cut their cake, and they ate great food. But as the sun was starting to set on the best day of his life, Kyle wanted his wife all to himself, and he whisked her away in his truck—which the guys had decorated with a JUST MARRIED sign on the bumper, along with half a dozen beer cans on the back that dragged behind them as they drove away from the venue with everyone watching them go.

"Where to now, husband?" Ella said as she ran her hand up his thigh and glanced at him with a sexy smile that made his dick twitch in his slacks.

He grinned right back at her as he turned onto the highway. "Anxious to get started on the honeymoon, Sunshine?"

"Maybe," she teased as her fingers danced

over the bulge in his pants. Then she frowned as she realized the direction he was driving. "But this isn't the way to the bed-and-breakfast we were going to stay at tonight."

Tomorrow, they were flying to Aruba for a week for the real honeymoon and vacation and time alone that the two of them desperately needed. "No, it's not. I want to take you to see one of the most spectacular views you'll ever see."

"I'm looking at him right now," she said with a sassy wink.

Another twenty minutes outside of Woodmont and off a back road, Kyle pulled up to a huge expanse of land. In the distance, the sun was almost gone, and the two of them got out of the vehicle to watch, hand in hand, as rich hues of pink, purple, and blues stretched across the horizon.

"A beautiful way to end a perfect day," Ella said appreciatively.

"This is how I want to end every day with you," he said, giving her soft hand a squeeze in his.

She tipped her head curiously at him. "Watching a sunset?"

He nodded. "Yes. Specifically, this one.

Right here. Like this."

She laughed, and he couldn't blame her for the odd look she was giving him. "It's kind of far to drive to every night, don't you think?"

Kyle turned toward her and took both of her hands in his, wanting to make sure she understood what he was about to say. "It won't be far to drive to it at all, because this is where we're going to live."

Her breath caught, and her eyes grew round. "What?"

Confusion. Disbelief. Hope. It all flitted across her expression and told him he'd made the right decision to buy this plot of land. "This right here is your wedding gift, Sunshine," he said, smiling at her. "Over ten acres of land. I'm going to build you a house here. And it's going to be big so we can fill it with love and laughter and at least three kids and a dog and a cat. Hell, we've got so much land you can have a farm if you want," he added teasingly. "The best part is, it's only twenty minutes away from your store, and twenty minutes closer to the city for my work."

"Nice compromise, City Boy," she said in a voice that reflected the tears shimmering in her eyes.

"Right?" He laughed for a moment, then grew serious as he reached out and skimmed his fingers along her pretty face. A face he was going to be lucky enough to look at for the rest of his days. "But it honestly doesn't matter where we live. *You* are my home, Ella. Where you are, that will always be home to me."

She closed her eyes and rubbed her cheek against the palm of his hand. "I'm not sure I deserve you."

"Yes, you do. We deserve each other." He tipped her chin up and kissed her, slow and sensual and packed with emotion. "I love you, Mrs. Coleman," he murmured against her lips.

"And I love you, Mr. Coleman," she whispered, then grinned against his mouth. "Now let's go consummate this marriage."

It was an order Kyle wasn't about to refuse.

Thank you for reading WELL BUILT. We hope you enjoyed Kyle and Ella's story! We would appreciate it if you would help others enjoy this book by leaving a review at your preferred e-tailer. Thank you!

Up next, Connor Prescott in ROCK SOLID.

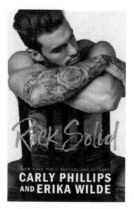

Connor Prescott doesn't do one night stands (yes, ladies, he's an anomaly) so when he meets a beautiful woman during a snowed in night at the airport who wants to forget her heartache, he makes an exception. Their night together is incendiary, and by morning Connor wants more . . . except his sexy stranger is gone. He's pretty sure he'll never see her again, until three and a half years later she finds *him*, and changes his entire world with three little words . . . *You're a daddy*.

Order ROCK SOLID today!

COMING NEXT FROM CARLY!

Rock Me

September 19, 2017

Bodyguard Bad Boys . . . Sexy, Hot, and oh so protective!

A pop star in danger. Her reluctant bodyguard. A past they can't deny.

Summer Michelle is on the verge of ultimate fame. Ben Hollander has sworn off mixing business with pleasure. But keeping his hands off of the sexy songstress is easier said than done and once the threat is neutralized, will she choose fame over love?

ROCK ME EXCERPT

THEY FILED INTO the room where Dan had already taken up lead position at the head of the table. When not working, their boss was a big believer in blowing off steam during off hours, hence the game room with the pool table, dart board, and during lunch, an endless supply of eats. Located in the Whitestone area of the Bronx, there was no better bodyguard agency to work for in the tri-state area of New York, New Jersey and Connecticut.

"Okay kids, time for new assignments," Dan said.

Ben rolled his shoulders, leaning his elbow on the table. "Let me have it, boss."

"You might not be so eager when you hear what it is but keep in mind, we are out of options. Everyone's on another assignment." Dan eyed him with a healthy dose of an apology in his gaze followed by his tough shit look.

The hair on the back of Ben's neck stood on end. "What's going on?"

"A little show and tell is in order for this assignment," Dan said, gesturing to the screen behind him. He pulled out his computer and tapped a few keys.

Up popped a photograph of Jade Glow, one of the world's most popular contemporary recording artists in the world. "Jade Glow needs an opening act and couldn't decide between two up and coming singers. Her solution? To give both women a chance to build their *star power* while she waits, watches audience reaction, and makes a decision."

Dan chose his words carefully. He always did. Which was why the words *star power* stood out like a beacon to Ben. Four years ago, he'd been a security guard on the set of the hit television show of the same name, where he'd met, fucked and then proceeded to be fucked over by one of the show's up and coming stars.

He'd not only had sex with one of the contestants, Summer Michelle, he'd violated his contract by doing so. Someone had turned him in but the producers made it clear to him – the word had leaked from Summer herself. Ben had lost his job for consorting with the talent, while she'd gone on to tie for runner up in the show. His current boss knew the whole sordid story but he believed in second chances and besides, Ben had come highly recommended from the firm he'd worked for prior to Dan's. He'd had to take a trial period while he earned his position and proved to his then-bosses he could be trusted to think smart on the job. Be a professional. Keep his dick in his pants. Not get taken in by a pretty face.

Ben's lesson had been learned the hard way.

"No. Fucking. Way." Another thing about Dan. He invited his people to speak their mind, which was why Ben had no problem expressing himself now. "If you are telling me I'm now bodyguard to Summer Michelle . . . that's a hell no."

Dan ran a hand over his cropped short, salt and pepper hair. "I'm not finished with the explanation, although now that you've put together who's involved . . ." Dan hit a key on the laptop and Summer's picture jumped onto the screen alongside a girl he remembered from the show as well, Tawny Renee.

Ben's visceral reaction to Summer's photo didn't bode well for this potential assignment. He hadn't seen Summer in years but looking at her was like a punch to the gut and a kick start to his groin all at the same time. The publicity photo accentuated her glossy black hair still long, still curling over her shoulders in a glorious silken wave. Her golden brown eyes stared back at him while her pink lips were glossed in a pretty pout. And he distinctly remembered having those same lips wrapped around his dick, while her tongue did her best to make him come.

Damn. How had fate landed her back in his lap?

Okay bad choice of words, he thought, and cringed.

"You with me?" Dan asked.

Beside them, Jared and Ava were silent, no doubt either enjoying his discomfort or uncomfortable themselves by the situation Ben now found himself in.

"I'm listening," Ben muttered to Dan.

The older man nodded. "Vague threats have come to Jade Glow's people regarding picking Summer for the opening act, so Orion Motors, the sponsor of her world tour, wants to hire protection for both women just to be safe."

"Are you giving me a choice of who I get to protect?" Ben asked. Neither option appealed. Tawny had been a spoiled brat with constant demands but for some reason, Summer had liked the other girl. The two had been friends. Maybe that should have been Ben's first clue to steer clear of Summer Michelle.

"No. There's no choice for you. We're the best in the business and Jade's people want us to look out for Summer, since the threats focused solely on her. Unfortunately we have no other bodyguards to offer, at least for the moment, so they hired another firm for Tawny. You going to be okay?"

Since he didn't have a choice, he nodded.

"Good. Everything else you need to know about the case is in the file," Dan went on. "Her itinerary is in there as well, so you'll know where to meet up with her later today. She has a series of events lined up over the next two weeks in Manhattan. You'll stick close."

"How close?" Ben asked warily. Some cases involved daytime surveillance only.

"Summer lives on the West side in a one bedroom walk up. No doorman. No protection. So we're talking twenty-four-seven cover."

Of course they were. Because why should he catch a break?

Summer Michelle had been Ben's undoing four years ago, but he was determined not only to keep his distance but to make certain that he was the one calling the shots this time around.

Order Rock Me Today!

COMING NEXT FROM ERIKA!

Turning up the Heat

September 19, 2017

Radio personality Kerri McCree really likes sex. Talking about sex, that is . . .

Kerri knows firsthand that you can hide a lot behind a microphone. Although she's earned a reputation for discussing every aspect of sex on her show, she's never had to back it up . . . until a sexy mystery caller proves to be even more irresistible in person.

Ian Carlisle is immediately intrigued by the sultry voice he hears on the late night radio show, and it doesn't take him long to arouse Kerri's imagination with his dirty talk. Now he's turning up the heat and seducing the rest of her. Their on-the-air chemistry sizzles and they heat up the airwaves, debating any and all provocative issues possible. As the ratings soar, so does the sexual tension.

But will Ian do when he discovers Kerri's not the sex expert she professes to be?

Order Turning up the Heat Today!

Sign up for Carly Phillips & Erika Wilde's Newsletters:

Carly's Newsletter
http://smarturl.it/CarlysNewsletter

Erika's Newsletter
http://smarturl.it/ErikaWildeNewsletter

ABOUT THE AUTHORS

CARLY PHILLIPS

Carly Phillips is the *N.Y. Times* and *USA Today* Bestselling Author of over 50 sexy contemporary romance novels featuring hot men, strong women and the emotionally compelling stories her readers have come to expect and love. Carly is happily married to her college sweetheart, the mother of two nearly adult daughters and three crazy dogs (two wheaten terriers and one mutant Havanese) who star on her Facebook Fan Page and website. Carly loves social media and is always around to interact with her readers. You can find out more about Carly at www.carlyphillips.com.

ERIKA WILDE

Erika Wilde is the author of the sexy Marriage Diaries series and The Players Club series. She lives in Oregon with her husband and two daughters, and when she's not writing you can find her exploring the beautiful Pacific Northwest. For more information on her upcoming releases, please visit website at www.erikawilde.com.